The Mystery of the Missing Necklace

The Fifth Adventure
in Enid Blyton's
celebrated series

Granada Publishing Limited
Published in 1967 by Dragon Books
3 Upper James Street, London W1R 4BP
Reprinted 1967, 1968, 1969, 1970, 1971 (twice), 1972

First published by Methuen & Co Ltd 1947
Copyright © Enid Blyton 1947
Made and printed in Great Britain by
C. Nicholls & Company Ltd
The Philips Park Press, Manchester
Set in Intertype Times

The Mystery of the Missing Necklace

Enid Blyton

Text illustrations by Mary Gernat

Dragon

"Hallo, Fatty! Jolly good, old boy."

Oh, for a Mystery!

Pip and Bets sat in their garden, in the very coolest place they could find. They had on sun-suits and nothing else, for the August sun was blazing hot.

"A whole month of the summer hols gone already!" said Pip. "And except that we've been away to the seaside for two weeks, absolutely nothing else has happened. Most boring."

"The boringest hols we've ever had," said Bets. "Not even the smell of a mystery to solve! And not even Larry, Daisy, Fatty, or Buster to play with – they've been away at the sea for ages!"

Larry and Daisy were friends of Pip and Bets, and so was Frederick – or Fatty as everyone called him. Buster was his Scottie dog, loved by all the children.

The five children called themselves the Five Find-Outers and Dog, because for the last four holidays they had tackled curious mysteries and solved them all – much to the annoyance of the village policeman, Mr. Goon.

"But now it seems as if you and I, Pip, are the only Find-Outers left," said Bets. "I don't feel as if the others will ever come back! Soon the hols will be over, you'll all be back at boarding-school again, except me, and we shan't solve any mystery at all these hols."

"There are still four weeks left, so cheer up, baby!" said Pip. "And the others come back this week – and I bet old Fatty will have heaps of new disguises to try out on us! We'll be on the look-out for him this time, though – and we jolly well won't be taken in!"

Bets laughed. She remembered how Fatty had disguised himself as a French boy, and deceived them all beautifully. And in the last holidays he had produced all kinds of disguises, which he wore with a red wig and eyebrows. There was no knowing what old Fatty would be up to next!

"But *this* time he won't deceive us," said Pip again. "I shall be very suspicious of any peculiar-looking stranger who tries to talk to me, or comes to call on us. I shall say to myself, 'It's you all right, Fatty,' and I shan't listen to a word!"

"Do you think there will be a mystery for us to solve these hols?" asked Bets. "I do so like looking for clues, and making out lists of Suspects, and crossing people off the list when we've made enquiries – and finding the real Suspect at the end!"

"We've been jolly lucky so far," said Pip, sitting up and looking round for the bottle of lemonade he had brought out. "We've been able to solve every single mystery. We can't always be successful, though. I don't expect even real detectives are always successful. Bets, you pig, you've finished the lemonade. Go and ask Gladys for some iced water."

Bets was too lazy to move. She rolled over out of Pip's reach, and yawned loudly. "I'm bored! I want the others to come back so that we can have games with them. I want a mystery – a really good one. And I want to solve it before Old Clear-Orf does!"

Old Clear-Orf was Mr. Goon the policeman. He told children and dogs to "clear-orf" whenever he saw them. He disliked all the Find-Outers intensely, and never

6

had a good word to say for them. Pip and Bets hadn't seen much of him in the summer holidays, and were very glad, for he had often been to their parents to complain of the behaviour of the Five Find-Outers. Bets was afraid of him, because when he lost his temper he shouted, and was very unpleasant indeed.

"Bets, didn't you hear me tell you to go in and fetch some iced water?" said Pip crossly. "Go on!"

"I'm not going to be ordered about by you," said Bets, rolling a bit farther away. "I suppose you order all the little boys about in your school, and then when you come home you think you can order me about too. Well, I shall soon be ten, and you're not to!"

"Don't you cheek me, young Bets!" said Pip, sitting up. "You're much younger than I am, and you've got to do as you're told! Go and get that iced water – or I'll catch you and give you a jolly good smacking."

"I think you're a horrid brother to have," said Bets. "I'd much rather have Fatty. He's always kind to me!"

"He wouldn't be, if you were his sister," said Pip. "He hasn't got any sisters – if he had, he'd know what a nuisance they are. Now – are you going to go and . . ."

"Yes, I'll get it!" said Bets, getting up, "but only because *I'm* thirsty, and *I* want some to drink, see? I don't mind bringing you out a little too, as I'm going to get some for myself, but I'm really going for myself, and . . ."

Pip pretended to be getting up, and Bets fled. If only the others would come back! She and Pip were getting tired of one another.

Bets hadn't long to wait before the others came back. In two days' time Larry, Daisy, Fatty, and Buster all turned up together, looking so brown that Pip and Bets had to gaze earnestly at them to make sure they really were their friends. Buster wasn't brown, of course – he was still jet-black, and he flung himself on Pip and Bets in joy and delight, barking and licking and whining as if he had gone mad.

"Buster, darling! You're fatter! Oh, Larry, I'm glad you're back! Daisy, you're terribly brown. And oh, Fatty – you've *grown!*"

Fatty certainly had grown in the last four months. He was still plump, but he was taller, taller even than Larry now, and much taller than Pip, who didn't seem to have grown at all in the last year.

"Hallo, every one!" he said, and Bets gave a cry of surprise.

"Fatty! You've got a different voice! It's a grown-up voice! Are you putting it on – disguising it, I mean?"

"No," said Fatty, pulling Bets' hair teasingly. "It's just broken, that's all."

"Who broke it?" said Bets, in alarm, and the others roared at her till their sides ached.

"She'll never be anything but a baby!" said Pip. "Never."

Bets looked so upset and puzzled that Fatty put his arm round her and gave her a squeeze. "Bets, don't be silly. You know that when they grow up, boys get deep voices like men's, don't you? Well, when boys' voices change like that we say that their voices *break* – that's all. We don't mean broken in half, or smashed to pieces!"

"Oh, Fatty – I don't know you with such a deep voice," said Bets, half-alarmed. "You don't sound the same. You *look* like Fatty – but you don't sound like him! I wish you had your old voice."

"Bets, you've no idea what a difference it makes to me, now I've got a proper grown-up voice," said Fatty earnestly. "It means that I can disguise myself as a grown-up instead of always like some kind of boy! It gives me much more scope – and I've got some fine grown-up disguises!"

Bets immediately changed her mind about not liking Fatty's new voice. More disguises! Now life would be exciting and thrilling and unexpected things would happen. Fatty would disguise himself as all kinds of grown-up people – the Find-Outers would have a simply gorgeous time. She stared at Fatty happily.

"Oh, Fatty! You've only been able to dress up as telegraph boys or butcher boys or messenger boys before! Now you can be all kinds of things – old men with beards – a postman – a dustman – a window-cleaner with a ladder – even a sweep! Oh, Fatty, do be all those things and let's see you!"

Every one laughed. "Give me a chance!" said Fatty. "I'm going to practise a bit these hols. I didn't have much chance whilst I was away, because Mother wouldn't let me take much luggage – but I don't mind telling you I'm going to collect a few things now! I've got taller too, so I can almost wear grown-ups' things. By the time our next mystery comes along I shall be able to tackle it in whatever disguise is necessary."

"You do sound grown-up," said Bets. "Doesn't he, everybody?"

"Well, as a matter of fact," said Fatty, swelling up a little with pride, "I'm the tallest boy in my form now, and you should just see the muscles in my arms. I'll show you!"

"Same old Fatty!" said Larry. "Best in everything, aren't you? Nobody to beat you!"

Fatty grinned and peeled off his shirt. He bent his arm and showed them how his muscles came up in a big lump. Bets looked on in awe, but Larry and Pip did not seem to be much impressed.

"Fair!" said Larry. "I've seen better ones on a boy of twelve!"

"Huh! You're jealous!" said Fatty, good-humouredly. "Now then – let's hear any Peterswood news, Pip and Bets. The village seemed pretty crowded when I came through it just now."

"Too jolly crowded for anything!" said Pip. "This hot weather is drawing the people to the river in their hundreds! We get motor-coaches all day long – and down by the river there are all sorts of shows to amuse the people when they get tired of the river, or it's raining."

"What sort of shows?" asked Fatty, lying down on the grass, and tickling Buster on his tummy. "Any good?"

"Not much," said Pip. "There's a Waxwork Show – pretty dull really – you know, figures made of wax, all dressed up – and there are those Bumping Motor-Cars – they're quite fun for the first two or three times you go in them. . . ."

"And a Hoopla game," said Bets. "You buy three wooden rings for twopence, and you try to throw them over any of the things arranged on a big round table – and if the ring goes right over anything, you can have whatever you've ringed. I like that game."

"You would!" said Pip. "She spends a whole shilling on hiring the wooden rings – and then wins a mouldy

10

little brooch worth a penny, that Mother can't bear and won't let her wear!"

"Well, Pip, you spent tenpence once, and you didn't win a thing!" began Bets hotly. But Fatty interrupted.

"Sounds as if Peterswood is going quite gay!" he said. "We'll have to make up a party and go down to all these shows one wet afternoon. If it ever *is* wet again!"

"Fatty, will you go in one of your new grown-up disguises?" asked Bets excitedly. "Oh, do! It would be lovely to see you acting like a grown-up, and taking everybody in!"

"I'll see," said Fatty. "I'd like to take in Old Clear-Orf, I must say! He's up to all my boy-disguises now – he'd see through them at once – but I bet he wouldn't see through a grown-up disguise!"

"What will you go as?" asked Daisy.

"Don't know," said Fatty. "And listen, all of you – if you can get any old things of your fathers' – you know, old hats they don't want, or boots, or even old coats – they'd come in mighty useful for me. I'm afraid if I take too many of my father's things, he'll be annoyed. Mother doesn't let him keep any of his old things, she gives them away – so he's only got rather newish clothes."

"We'll do what we can," promised Larry, and Pip nodded too. Anything to help old Fatty to disguise himself! Bets sighed with joy to think that Fatty was back again. Now life would really be exciting once more. And oh, if *only* a mystery turned up, how heavenly the rest of the hols would be!

Mr. Goon is Very Annoying

It was lovely to be all together again, day after day. The Five bathed in the river, went for long bicycle rides, lazed in the garden, squabbled, drank pints of iced drinks, and ate hundreds of ices. Buster liked both lemonade and ices and had his full share. He got rather fat and Pip teased him.

"You're too fat to go after rabbits, Buster!" he said. "Why, even a mouse would escape you now. You don't walk any more, you waddle. You don't breathe, you wheeze! You ..."

"Oh, don't tease him so," said Bets, who was always quite certain that Buster could understand every single word said to him. "He *doesn't* waddle. I bet if he saw Old Clear-Orf this very minute he'd be after him like a shot!"

"By the way, what's happened to Goon?" asked Fatty. "I saw him yesterday, in a great hurry and looking frightfully important."

"Probably solving some Mystery we don't know anything about," said Larry gloomily. "There have been a lot of burglaries lately, and perhaps Goon is getting at the bottom of them.

"Yes – but the burglaries haven't been in his district," said Fatty. "They've mostly been miles away. I've read about them in the paper. Lady Rexham's jewels were stolen only last week – and somebody else's famous diamonds the week before. It's a clever gang of thieves

– but they're not working this district, as far as I know."

"I wish they were!" said Bets. "Then we could catch them. You could put on one of your new disguises, Fatty, and track them down."

"It's not as easy as all that, little Bets, and you know it!" said Fatty, with a laugh. "You just think of all the difficulties we had in our other mysteries."

"We haven't seen you in any grown-up disguise yet, Fatty," said Daisy. "Do put one on, so that we can spot you in it, if we can."

"I've been practising in my bedroom," said Fatty. "I don't want to try anything out on you till I'm perfect. I'll try it on you when I'm ready, I promise. And I'll give my second-best propelling-pencil to any one of you that spots me first, see?"

"Oooh, Fatty – the pencil that can write in lead, or in red, or in blue?" said Bets. "Can you really spare it?"

"I'll certainly give it to any of the Find-Outers if they're bright enough to spot me in my first grown-up disguise," said Fatty. "It's a bargain!"

"I bet I'll spot you first," said Larry. "The girls won't, I'm sure. Pip might – but I'll be first!"

"We'll have to leave Buster behind when we try to do the spotting," said Pip. "Or he'll simply rush up to you and bark madly to tell every one it's you!"

"Yes. Buster's out of this," said Fatty, and Buster cocked up his ears at his name. "Sorry, Buster, old boy – but tomorrow you must stay at home with the cat."

"Oh, Fatty – are you going to dress up *tomorrow*?" asked Bets, in delight. "Really tomorrow? Well, you won't deceive *me*! I shall look at every one with an eagle eye!"

"Right," said Fatty. "But all the same – I have a feeling that my propelling-pencil will still be safely in my pocket tomorrow night! You may be quite good Find-Outers – but I'm a bit cleverer than any of you!"

"You're certainly best at boasting!" said Larry. "That trumpet of yours must be quite worn out by now."

"What trumpet?" said Bets, in curiosity. "I've never seen Fatty with a trumpet."

"No, but surely you've heard him blowing his own trumpet?" said Larry. "It's deafening at times! It's . . ."

And then Fatty sat up and flung himself on Larry and there was a great deal of shouting and yelling and squealing, with Buster plunging into the middle of the brawl and getting wildly excited too.

Mrs. Hilton, Pip's mother, appeared. "Children! You do know I've visitors in the garden, surely? If you want to yell and squeal and fight, will you go somewhere else? What about a nice walk?"

"Oh *Mother* – it's too hot for a walk!" groaned Pip.

"Well, I should have thought it was much too hot to fight," said Mrs. Hilton disapprovingly. "Really, Larry and Frederick, you look very dirty and untidy!"

"Sorry, Mrs. Hilton," said Fatty meekly, and Larry tried to smooth his hair down. "We'll go for a walk. I forgot you had people to tea in the garden. I really do apologize."

Fatty had marvellous manners with grown-up people, and Mrs. Hilton began to smile again. "Go down to the dairy and get yourselves an ice-cream each," she said. "That will get rid of you for a bit. Here's the money, Pip."

"Oh thanks, Mother," said Pip, and they all got up, pleased. It was the fourth ice-cream that day, but it

14

didn't seem worth while mentioning that to Mrs. Hilton. Fatty's mother had already provided ice-creams and so had Larry's, and Fatty had generously given them one each as well. Now this was the fourth lot. Goody!

They walked sedately down the garden and round the drive to the gates. They went to the dairy, which made real cream-ices that were most delicious, and sat down at the little table in the window to eat them.

Mr. Goon passed by on his bicycle as they sat there. He pedalled furiously, his face hot and red.

"Spot of hard work for Goon," said Fatty, letting a cold spoonful of ice-cream slide as slowly down his throat as possible. "Looks busy, doesn't he?"

Before they had finished their ices, Goon came pedalling back again, as furiously as before. The police-station was just opposite the dairy, and the children watched the policeman go smartly up the steps. Then they saw his head behind the frosted window-pane of one of the rooms in the police-station, talking to somebody else. Goon was talking the most and was nodding vigorously.

"Never seen Goon so busy before!" said Fatty, in astonishment. "Do you think he's really got a case to work on – a mystery to solve that we don't know anything about?"

"Golly, here he comes again!" said Pip, as Goon scuttled out of the police-station, buttoning a big sheaf of papers into his breast-pocket. "He's simply bursting with importance."

"He's feeling jolly pleased about something," said Fatty. "I *should* be mad if something had cropped up in Peterswood whilst I've been away, and we don't know anything about it!"

Goon jumped on to his bicycle and pedalled away again. It was maddening to sit there and watch him so busy and important and not know why. Fatty felt as if he was bursting with curiosity.

"He's on to something!" he said. "He really is. I know that look on his face. We *must* find out what it is!"

"Well, you find out then," said Larry. "And if he tells you, you'll be lucky! It's what Goon has dreamed of for months — a mystery all to himself, that the Five Find-Outers don't know anything about!"

"I can't bear it!" said Fatty, and let the last spoonful of ice-cream go down his throat. Then he looked dismayed. "Oh I say — do you know, I was so puzzled about Old Clear-Orf and his mystery that I ate that ice-cream without tasting it. What a fearful waste. I'll have to have another."

The others looked at him. "There's no more money," said Pip. "We spent it all."

"I've got some," said Fatty, and dug his hand into his pocket. He always had plenty of money, much to the envy of the others, who had pocket-money each Saturday and had to make that do for the week, like most children. But Fatty had plenty of rich relations, who seemed to pour money into his pockets in a most lavish way.

"Mother says it's bad for you to have so much money," said Pip. "She's always saying that."

"It probably is bad for me," said Fatty, "but I'm not going round telling my relations to stop giving me tips. Now, who wants another ice-cream? Bets?"

"Oh, Fatty, I couldn't," sighed Bets sadly. "I'd love to, but I know I can't. I feel a bit sick already."

"Well, go outside," said Pip unfeelingly. "No thanks,

Fatty. I don't feel sick, but I shan't eat any supper if I have another, and then Mother will stop all ice-creams for a week, or something awful."

Larry and Daisy said they couldn't possibly eat another either, so Fatty had a second one all by himself, and this time he said he tasted every spoonful, so it wasn't wasted as the first one had been.

Mr. Goon came back on his bicycle, just as the children left the shop. "There he is again!" said Fatty admiringly. "I've never seen him move so quickly. Good evening, Mr. Goon!"

Mr. Goon was just getting off his bicycle to go into the police-station again. He glanced at Fatty, and took no notice of him. Fatty was annoyed.

"You seem extremely busy, Mr. Goon," he said. "Solving another mystery, I suppose? Nice to get the old brains to work, isn't it? I could do with a bit of that myself, after lazing away most of these holidays."

"Oh? You got some brains then?" said Mr. Goon sarcastically. "That's good hearing, that is. But I'm busy now, and can't stop to talk about your brains, Master Frederick. There's Big Things going on, see, and I've got plenty to do without wasting my time talking to you."

"Big Things?" said Fatty, suddenly interested. "What, another Mystery, Mr. Goon? I say – that's . . ."

"Yes, another Mystery," said Mr. Goon, almost bursting with importance. "And I'm IN CHARGE of it, see? I'm the one that's tackling it, not you interfering kids. And not a word do I tell you about it, not one word. It's Secret and Important, and it's a Matter for the police!"

"But Mr. Goon – you know how we . . ." began Fatty anxiously; but the policeman, feeling for once that he

17

had got the better of Fatty, interrupted loftily.

"All I know about you is that you're a conceited, interfering kid what ought to be put in his place and kept there – you and your nasty barking dog! This here case is mine, and I'm already getting on with it, and what's more I'll get Promotion over this as sure as my name is Theophilus Goon," said the policeman, marching up the steps to the police-station. "You clear-orf now!"

"What a blow!" muttered poor, disappointed Fatty, as Goon disappeared through the door. He and the others walked home slowly, discussing all that Clear-Orf had said.

"To think of that fat policeman at work on a perfectly gorgeous new mystery that we don't know a thing about!" said Fatty, looking so miserable that Bets put her arm through his. "It's maddening. And the worst of it is that I simply don't see how we are going to find out a thing, if Goon won't tell us."

"Even Buster's upset about it," said Bets. "He's got his tail right down. So have you, poor Fatty. Never mind – you're going to try out your grown-up disguise tomorrow – that will be a bit of excitement for you, Fatty. And for us too!"

"Yes, it will," said Fatty, cheering up a little. "Well – I'll be getting back home now. Got to practise my disguise a bit before I try it out on you all tomorrow. So long!"

Fatty Disguises Himself

Next morning Larry had a note from Fatty.

"Go down to the side-shows by the river this afternoon. I'll meet you somewhere in disguise. Bet you won't know me!

"Fatty."

Larry showed the note to Pip and Bets when he went to see them that morning. Bets was thrilled. "What *will* Fatty be dressed in? I bet I'll know him! Oh, I can't wait for this afternoon to come!"

Larry's mother gave him some money to spend at the side-shows when she heard they were all going there that afternoon. They set off at two o'clock, ready to spot Fatty, no matter how well he was disguised.

As they walked down the village street an old bent man came shuffling up towards them. He stooped badly and dragged his feet, which were in old boots, the toes cracked and the heels worn down. He wore a straggly sandy-grey beard, and had shaggy grey eyebrows, and he looked extremely dirty. His coat sagged away from his bent shoulders, and his corduroy trousers were tied up with string at the knees.

His hat was too large for him and was crammed down over his head. He had a stick in his hand and used it to help himself along. He shuffled to a bench and sat down in the sun, sniffing loudly.

"That's Fatty! I know it is!" said Bets. "It's just the sort of disguise he'd put on. Isn't he clever?"

The old man took a pipe out of his pocket and began to stuff it with tobacco.

"Fancy Fatty even thinking of bringing a pipe!" said Pip. "I bet he's watched his father stuffing tobacco into his pipe. Golly – don't say he's even going to smoke it!"

Apparently he was! Great puffs of rather evil-smelling, strong smoke came wafting out from the old man. The children stared. "I shouldn't have thought Fatty *could* smoke," said Larry. "He oughtn't to. He's not old enough. But I suppose if he's in disguise . . ."

The old fellow sniffed loudly and then wiped his hand across his nose. Bets giggled. "Oh dear! Fatty is really simply marvellous. I do think he is. He must have been practising that awful sniffle for ages."

Larry went over to the old man and sat down beside him. "Hallo, Fatty!" he said. "Jolly good, old boy! But we all recognized you at once!"

The old man took absolutely no notice at all. He went on puffing at his pipe and clouds of the smoke floated into Larry's face.

"Fatty! Stop it! You'll make yourself sick if you smoke like that!" said Larry. The others joined him and sat there, giggling. Pip gave the old man a punch in the ribs.

"Hey, Fatty! You can stop pretending now. We know it's you!"

The old man felt the punch and looked round indignantly, his eyes almost hidden under his shaggy eyebrows. He moved a little way away from Larry and Pip and went on smoking.

"Fatty! Shut up smoking and talk to us, idiot!" said Pip. The old man took his pipe out of his mouth, put his hand behind his ear, and said "Wassat?"

"He's pretending to be deaf now!" said Bets, and giggled again.

"Ah?" said the old man, looking puzzled. "Wassat?"

"What does 'Wassat' mean?" asked Bets.

"It means 'What's that' of course," said Larry. "Hey, Fatty, stop it now. Give up, and tell us we're right. We all spotted you at once."

"Wassat?" said the old man again and put his hand behind his ear once more. It was a very peculiar ear, large and flat and purple red. Bets gazed at it and then nudged Daisy.

"Daisy! We've made a frightful mistake! It's not Fatty. Look at his ears!"

Every one gazed at the old fellow's ears. No – not even Fatty could make his ears go like that. And they were not false ears either. They were quite real, not very clean, and remarkably hairy. In fact, they were most unpleasant ears.

"Golly! It *isn't* Fatty!" said Pip, gazing at the ears. "What *must* the old man think of us?"

"Wassat?" said the old man again, evidently extremely puzzled at the children's familiar behaviour towards him.

"Well, thank goodness the poor old thing is deaf," said Daisy, feeling ashamed of their mistake. "Come on Larry, come on, Pip, We've made an idiotic mistake! How Fatty would laugh if he knew!"

"He's probably hiding somewhere around and grinning to himself like anything," said Pip. They left the

21

puzzled old man sitting on his bench and went off down the street again. They met the baker, and Bets gave him a long and piercing stare, wondering if he could by any chance be Fatty. But he wasn't. He was much too tall.

Then they met the window-cleaner, and as he was rather plump, and just about Fatty's height, they all went and pretended to examine his barrow of ladders and pails, taking cautious glances at him to find out whether or not *he* could be Fatty in disguise.

"Here! What's the matter with you kids?" said the window-cleaner. "Haven't you ever seen ladders and pails before? And what are you giving me them looks for? Anything wrong with me today?"

"No," said Larry hurriedly, for the window-cleaner sounded rather annoyed. "It's just that – er – these sliding ladders – er – are rather interesting!"

"Oh, *are* they?" said the window-cleaner disbelievingly. "Well, let me tell you this . . ."

But the children didn't listen to what he had to tell them. They hurried off, rather red in the face.

"I say! We shall get into trouble if we go squinting at every one to find out if they really are Fatty," said Larry. "We'll have to look at people a bit more carefully – I mean, without them knowing it."

"There he is – I'm sure of it!" said Bets suddenly, as they went over the level-crossing to the river-side, where the side-shows were. "Look – that porter with the moustache. That's Fatty, all right!"

The porter was wheeling a barrow up the platform, and the others stood and admired him. "He wheels it exactly like a *real* porter," said Bets. "Why do porters always wear waistcoats and no coats at railway stations?

I'm sure that's Fatty. It's just the way he walks. And he's plump like Fatty too."

She raised her voice and hailed the porter. "Hey, Fatty! Fatty!"

The porter turned round. He set his barrow down on the ground and walked towards them, looking angry.

"Who are you calling Fatty?" he demanded, his face red under his porter's cap. "You hold your tongue, you cheeky kids!"

The children stared at him. "It *is* Fatty," said Bets. "Look, that's just how his hair sticks out when he wears a hat. Fatty! We know it's you!"

"Now you look here!" said the porter, coming nearer, "if you wasn't a little girl I'd come over and shake you good and proper. Calling me names! You ought to be ashamed of yourself, you did!"

"It *isn't* Fatty, you idiot," said Pip angrily to Bets. "Fatty isn't as short in the arms. *Now* you've got us into trouble!"

But very luckily for them, a train came thundering in at that moment and the porter had to run to open and shut doors and see to luggage. The children hastily left the level-crossing and ran down to the river.

"You *stupid*, Bets! You'll get us all into trouble if you keep on imagining every one is Fatty," said Pip. "Calling out 'Fatty' like that – especially as the porter *was* fat. He must have thought you were disgustingly rude."

"Oh dear – yes, I suppose it did sound awfully rude," said Bets, almost in tears. "But I did think it was Fatty. I'll be more careful next time, Pip."

They came to the side-shows, which made a kind of

Fair alongside the river road. There was a Roundabout, the Hoopla game, the Bumping Motor-Cars, and the Waxwork Show. The children looked at the people crowding in and out of the Fair, and tried to see anyone that might be Fatty.

Bets was scared now to recognize any one as Fatty. She kept seeing people she thought might be Fatty and followed them around till she knew they weren't. The others did the same. Some people saw that they were being followed and didn't like it. They turned and glared.

"What you doing, keeping on my heels like this?" one man snapped at Larry. "Think I'm going to give you money for the Roundabout?"

Larry went red and slipped away. He imagined Fatty somewhere near, tickled to death to see the Find-Outers trying in vain to spot him. Where *could* he be?

"I think I've found him!" whispered Bets to Pip, catching hold of his arm. "He's the man selling the Roundabout tickets! He's just like Fatty, only he's got a black beard and thick black hair, and gold ear-rings in his ears, and an almost black face."

"Well, he doesn't sound 'just like Fatty' to *me*!" said Pip scornfully. "I'm tired of your spotting the wrong people, Bets. Where's this fellow?"

"I told you. Selling Roundabout tickets," said Bets, and though Pip felt quite certain that not even Fatty would be allowed to sell Roundabout tickets, he went to see. The man flashed a grin at him and held up a bunch of tickets.

"A lovely ride!" he chanted. "A lovely ride on the Roundabout. Only sixpence for a lovely ride!"

Pip gave the roundabout man a cheeky grin

Pip went and bought a ticket. He looked hard at the man, who gave him another cheeky grin. Pip grinned back.

"So it *is* you!" he said. "Jolly good, Fatty!"

"What you talking about?" said the Roundabout-man in surprise. "And who are you calling Fatty?"

Pip didn't like to say any more somehow, though he really was quite certain it was Fatty. He got on the Roundabout, chose a lion that went miraculously up and down as well as round and round, and enjoyed his ride.

He winked at the ticket-man as he got off and the man winked back. "Funny kid, aren't you?" said the man. Pip went to the others. "I've found Fatty," he said. "At least, I suppose it was Bets who did, really. It's the man who sells the tickets for the Roundabout."

"Oh no it isn't," said Larry. "Daisy and I have found Fatty too. It's the man who stands and shouts to people to come and have a go at the Hoopla. See – over there!"

"But it *can't* be!" said Pip. "He'd never be allowed to have a job like that. No, you're wrong. I don't think *that* can be Fatty."

"Well, and *I* don't think the Roundabout ticket-man is right, after all," said Bets unexpectedly. "I know I *did* think so. But I don't any more. His feet are much too small. He's got silly little feet. Fatty's got enormous feet. However much you disguise yourself you can't make big feet into small ones!"

"I bet Fatty could!" said Daisy. "He's a marvel. But I still think Fatty's the Hoopla-man – the one who shouts to people to come and try."

"And *I* think he's the ticket-man at the Roundabout," said Pip, obstinately. "Well – we'll see. We'll have some fun, get tea over there, and wait for Fatty to show himself in his own good time!"

Fun at the Fair

Having more or less decided the question of Fatty's disguise, though Bets was very doubtful indeed, the four children had some fun.

Bets bought some of the wooden Hoopla rings from the man that Larry and Daisy were certain was Fatty in disguise, and managed to ring a dear little clock. She was really delighted. She held out her hand for the clock, her eyes shining with joy. "It will do nicely for my bedroom mantelpiece," she said happily.

"Sorry," said the Hoopla-man. "The ring didn't go quite over the clock, Miss."

"But it *did*," said poor Bets. "It did. It didn't even touch the clock. It was the best throw I've ever done!"

"You didn't ring it properly, Miss," said the man. The other Hoopla-man, that Larry and Daisy thought was Fatty, looked on, and said nothing. Daisy, certain that it *was* Fatty, appealed to him, sorry to see little Bets being cheated out of the cheap little clock.

"She *did* win it, didn't she? Make this man let her have it!"

"Sorry, Miss. She didn't ring it properly," said that man too. And then Bets walked off, dragging the others with her. "*Now* do you think that man is Fatty?" she said fiercely. "*He* would have let me have the clock at once! Fatty is never unkind. He can't be Fatty!"

"Well – he might *have* to say a thing like that," argued Larry. "The other man might have got angry with him and given him a punch. I still think it's Fatty."

They went on the Roundabout, and in the Bumping Cars. Pip took Bets, and Larry went with Daisy, and with many squeals and yells they crashed into one another, and shook themselves and the little cars almost to pieces. It really was fun.

"Now let's go into the Waxwork Show," said Larry.

"Oh, it's too hot," said Daisy. "Really it is. Besides, I don't much like waxwork figures – they scare me a bit – they look so real, and yet they never even blink!"

"*I* want to see them," said Bets, who had never been inside a Waxwork Show in her life, and was longing to. "They've got Queen Elizabeth in there, all dressed up beautifully, and Napoleon, with his hand tucked into his waistcoat, and Nelson with one arm and one eye, and . . ."

"Oh well, let's go in and see all these wonderful persons," said Daisy. "But it's a marvel to me they don't all melt in this weather. I feel as if I'm melting myself. We'd better have ice-creams after this."

They paid their money and went in. The show was in a small hall. A red-headed boy took their money, scratching his head violently with one hand as he handed them tickets with the other. Bets stared at him. Could *he* be Fatty? Fatty had a red-headed wig and eye-brows, and he could put freckles all over his face, just like the ones this boy had. But Fatty had said he would be in a *grown-up* disguise – so he couldn't be this dirty-looking boy. Still – Bets couldn't help staring hard at him.

28

The boy put out his tongue at her.

"Stare away!" he said. "Never seen red hair before, I suppose!"

Bets went red and joined the others. All round the little hall, arranged on steps that raised each row of figures up behind the others, were the wax people. They stood there, still and silent, fixed looks on their pink faces, staring without blinking.

Pip and Larry liked them, but the two girls felt uncomfortable to have so many strange figures looking at them.

"There's Queen Elizabeth!" said Pip, pointing to a very grand-looking wax figure at the end of the little hall. "And there's Sir Walter Raleigh putting down his cloak for her to walk on. They're jolly good."

"What grand clothes she wears," said Bets, "and I like her big ruff. And look at all her beautiful jewellery. I'm surprised people don't steal it!"

"Pooh! All bought at Woolworth's!" said Pip. "I say – here's Nelson. I didn't know he was such a little chap."

"Oh – and here's Winston Churchill," said Bets in delight. She had a terrific admiration for this great statesman, and kept a photo of him on her mantelpiece. "With his cigar and all. He looks the best of the lot!"

"Look – there's a girl selling sweets," said Larry suddenly, winking at Pip. "Here, Bets, go and buy some chocolate for us." He gave the little girl some money and she went to the sweet-girl, who stood nearby with a tray of bags and boxes.

"I'll have some chocolate, please," said Bets, and held out her money. The girl didn't take it. She looked steadily over Bets' head and said nothing.

"SOME CHOCOLATE, PLEASE," said Bets loudly,

thinking that perhaps the girl was deaf. The girl took absolutely no notice at all, and Bets was puzzled.

Then she heard the others exploding behind her, and guessed in a flash the trick they had played. "Oh! This girl is a waxwork too! You beasts! I've been trying to buy chocolate from a waxwork figure."

"Oh, Bets! Anyone can take you in, simply anyone!" said Pip, almost crying with laughter. "To think you're one of the Find-Outers, too! Why, you can't even spot when somebody is a waxwork!"

Bets hardly knew whether to cry or to laugh, but fortunately she decided to laugh. "Oh dear! I really did think she was a proper person. Look at that horrid red-headed boy over there laughing at me!"

They examined all the wax figures closely. There were a good many of them. Among them was a policeman rather like Mr. Goon, but taller and not so fat.

"I'd like to stand Old Clear-Orf in here!" said Pip, with a giggle. "He looks just about as stolid and stupid sometimes. And I say – look at this postman. He's quite good, except for his idiotic grin."

It was really very hot in the Waxwork Show and the children were glad to go out. The red-headed boy at the entrance put out his tongue at Bets again, and she tried not to look.

"What a horrid boy!" she said. "I can't think how I thought he could be Fatty. Fatty wouldn't behave like that, even in disguise."

"Let's go and have some tea," said Daisy. "Look, this place has got ices and home-make cakes."

"Cakes and an iced lemonade for me," said Pip. "I'll have an ice later if I can manage it. I wish old Fatty could join us. Wonder if he's looking on at us, in his

30

disguise. I'm sure he's the ticket-man at the Round-about. That man's mop of curly black hair is too good to be true."

They had a very nice tea, and ate twenty-four cakes between them. They finished up with ices, washed down by a rather sweet lemonade, and then felt able to go out into the sun once more.

"Let's go and sit down by the river," said Bets. "It will be cooler there. There's always a breeze by the water!"

They made their way out of the Fair. Bets suddenly caught sight of a lovely patch of gay colour, and she stopped. "Pip! Look at those air-balloons! I do love a balloon. Have you got enough money to buy me one?"

"Don't be a baby," said Pip. "Fancy wanting a balloon like any three-year-old kid!"

"Well, I do," said Bets obstinately. They all went over to where the old woman sat, holding her bunch of gay balloons. She was a shapeless old dame, with a red shawl over her shoulders and head, though the day was hot. Untidy hair hung in wisps over her brown, wrinkled face, but she had surprisingly bright eyes.

"Balloon, young sir?" said she to Pip, in a cracked old voice.

"No thanks," said Pip. But Bets pulled his arm.

"Oh, do buy me one, Pip. Oh, I wish Fatty was here. He'd buy me one. They're so pretty!"

"Well, but they're sixpence each!" said Pip, looking at the price label hanging from the string of balloons. "Sixpence! It's robbery. No, I can't lend you sixpence for that. Mother would think I was mad."

"She can have one for half-price," croaked the old woman kindly. Bets looked at Pip.

31

"Oh, all right," he said, and pulled out three pennies. "But mind you give me the money back when you get home, Bets."

"Oh thank you, Pip," said Bets, and took the money. She looked at all the gay balloons, swaying gently in the breeze, and couldn't make up her mind which one to buy. The reds were so nice and bright, the greens were so pretty, the blues were like the sky, the yellows were like sunshine – oh, which should she have?

"Well, come on after us when you've made up your mind," said Pip impatiently. "We're not going to stand here all evening waiting for you, Bets."

The others went off to the river-bank. Bets stared at the lovely balloons.

"Pretty, aren't they, young miss?" said the old woman. "You take your time in choosing. I don't mind!"

Bets thought what a kind old woman she was. "It was so nice of you to let me have one at half-price," she said. "Really it was. Do you make a lot of money, selling balloons?"

"Not much," said the old dame. "But enough for an old lady like me."

Bets chose a blue balloon and the old woman held out her hand for the money. It was a very dirty hand, and it closed over the money quickly. Bets wondered why all the Fair people had such dirty hands and faces.

Then she noticed something that made her stare. The old woman's hand was certainly extremely dirty – but the nails on it were remarkably clean! Much cleaner than Bets' own nails!

"How queer!" thought Bets, still staring at the clean, well-kept nails. "Why should this old woman keep her

32

nails so clean, and her hands so dirty?"

Bets then looked hard at the old woman's dirty brown face, all wrinkled up. She looked into the surprisingly bright, twinkling eyes – and she saw that they were Fatty's eyes! Yes, there wasn't an atom of doubt about it – they were Fatty's own bright, intelligent eyes!"

"Oh, Fatty!" whispered Bets. "Oh, it really is you, isn't it? Oh, do say it is?"

The old woman looked round quickly to make sure no one was listening.

"Yes. It's me all right," said Fatty, unwrinkling his face as if by magic, and straightening his bent back. "Jolly good disguise, isn't it? But HOW did you know it was me, Bets? You're too cute for anything!"

"Sh! There's somebody coming," whispered Bets. "I'll go. Where will you meet us?"

"Go home at six and I'll meet you somewhere," said Fatty hurriedly, and screwed his face up into all kinds of wrinkles again. Bets saw that he had cleverly painted the places where the wrinkles came, so that no one could possibly see that they were not always there. Fatty was simply marvellous!

"Don't tell the others!" said Fatty. "Keep it dark for a bit." Then he raised his voice and, in a feeble croak, called "Balloons! Sixpence each! Fine strong balloons!"

Bets went off, her eyes shining. She had found Fatty – and oh, *wasn't* he clever! He really, really was.

The Old Balloon-Woman

Bets went to join the others, very pleased with herself. Her blue balloon floated behind her, tugging at its string.

"Here she is at last!" said Pip. "We thought you were never coming, Bets. What's up with you? You look bursting with something."

"Do I?" said Bets. "Fancy that! By the way, I've a message from Fatty. We're to go home at six and he will meet us somewhere."

"Who gave you that message?" said Pip, at once.

"That's *my* secret," said Bets annoyingly.

"Did you speak to Fatty himself?" demanded Larry. "Is he the Hoopla-man?"

"I shan't tell you," said Bets. "I'm going to keep my secret for a bit!"

And she wouldn't say another word, which annoyed the others very much. Fancy young Bets knowing something *they* didn't know!

At six o'clock they made their way back through the Fair, across the level-crossing, and up the lane from the river. Sitting on a bench, with her balloons, was the old Balloon-woman, waiting for them. She got up as they came.

"Balloons!" said she. "Strong balloons!"

"No thanks," said Pip, and walked on. The old woman walked with him. "Buy a balloon!" she said, "Just to help me, young sir!"

"No thanks," said Pip again, and walked a little

faster. But the old dame could walk surprisingly fast too. She kept up quite easily with Pip!

"*Do* buy a balloon!" she said, her voice cracking queerly.

How long she would have pestered Pip nobody knew – but Bets suddenly exploded into a series of helpless giggles that took the others by surprise. They stared at her.

"What *is* the matter?" said Pip, exasperated.

"Oh dear!" gasped Bets. "Oh dear – I'm sorry. But I can't help it. It's all so f-f-f-funny!"

"*What's* funny?" shouted Pip. And then he stared – for the old Balloon-woman, pulling her skirts above her knees, and showing sand-shoes and bare legs, was doing a lively jig in front of him and round him, making peculiar noises all the time.

"Don't, Fatty, don't! I shall die of laughter!" said Bets, holding her aching sides.

The others stared as if their eyes were about to fall out. "What – it's *Fatty*?" said Pip. "*Fatty*! It isn't. I can't believe it!"

But it was, of course. As soon as Fatty "unscrewed" his face, as Bets called it, and got rid of his lines and wrinkles, every one could see quite well it was Fatty.

Larry and Daisy were speechless. So Fatty hadn't been the Hoopla-man, or the Roundabout-man either. He was the old Balloon-woman instead. Trust Fatty to think out a disguise that nobody would guess!

Or had little Bets guessed it? The others looked at her smiling face. Larry dragged the Balloon-woman to a wayside seat, and they all sat down.

"Is it really you, Fatty?" said Larry. The old woman nodded.

"Of course! Golly, this disguise must be super if I could take you all in as well as that!"

"Did Bets guess?" demanded Pip.

"She did," said Fatty. "She suddenly guessed when she was buying her balloon, and you had all gone off without her."

"But how did she guess?" said Pip, annoyed.

"Goodness knows!" said Fatty. "How *did* you guess, young Bets?"

"Oh, Fatty – it was such a silly thing – I don't really like to tell you," said Bets. "I'm sure you'll think it was a silly way to guess."

"Go on – tell me," said Fatty, with much interest.

"Well, Fatty – you see, you had very dirty hands, like all the rest of the Fair people," said Bets. "But I couldn't help seeing that you had nice, clean nails – and it did seem to me a bit funny that somebody with dirty hands should bother to keep their nails so clean."

"Well, I'm blessed!" said Fatty, looking down at his dirty hands, and examining the well-kept nails. "Who would have thought of any one noticing that? Very very careless of me not to get some dirt into my nails when I made my hands filthy. I never thought of it. Bets, you are very clever. Most intelligent."

"Oh, Fatty – not really," said Bets, glowing all over her face at such generous praise.

"Well, I must say I think it was jolly cute of young Bets to notice a thing like that," said Larry. "I really do. We all had a chance of noticing, because we all stood in front of you. But it was Bets who spotted it. Jolly good, Bets!"

"She wins my second-best propelling-pencil," said Fatty. "I'll give it to you when I get home, Bets. In fact

I'm not sure that I oughtn't to give you my best one. That was a really smart bit of work. Bright enough for a first-class detective!"

Daisy praised Bets too, but Pip was rather sulky. He was afraid his little sister would get swollen-headed. "If you say much more, Bets will want to be head of the Find-Outers," he said.

"Oh no, I shan't," said Bets happily. "I know it was only a bit of luck, really, Pip. You see, I actually put the pennies into Fatty's hands, and that's how I noticed the clean nails. Pip, I'll lend you the propelling-pencil *whenever* you want it. See?"

That was so like Bets. Not even a cross elder brother like Pip could sulk for long with Bets. He grinned at her.

"Thanks, Bets. You're a good Find-Outer, and a good little sport too!"

"I say – look out – here's Goon!" suddenly said Larry, in a low voice. "Better pretend we're not with Fatty, or Goon will wonder why we are hob-nobbing with an old Fair woman!"

So they all got up, and left Fatty behind on the seat, with his string of balloons bobbing over his head. Mr. Goon was on his bicycle as usual. He pretended not to notice the children at all. He always seemed busy and important these days!

But he got off his bicycle when he saw the old woman. Fatty was drooping over, pretending to be asleep.

"Here, you!" said Goon. "Move on! And where's your licence to sell balloons?"

The others heard this, and looked alarmed. Did you have to have a licence to peddle balloons? They were sure Fatty hadn't got one.

Fatty took no notice, but gave a gentle snore. Mr. Goon shook the shoulder of the Balloon-woman, and Fatty pretended to awake with a jerk.

"Where's your licence?" said Goon. He was always rude and arrogant to people like the old Balloon-woman.

"What did you say, sir?" said Fatty, in a whining voice. "Want to buy a balloon, sir? What colour do you fancy?"

"I don't want a balloon," said Goon angrily. "I want to see your licence."

"Oh, ah, my licence?" said Fatty, and began to pat all over his extremely voluminous skirts, as if to find where a licence would possibly be hidden. "Somewhere about, sir, somewhere about. If you can just wait a few minutes, kind sir, I'll find it in the pocket of one of my petticoats. An old woman like me, sir, she wants plenty of petticoats. Sleeping out under hedges is cold, sir, even on a summer night."

"Gah!" said Goon rudely, mounted his bicycle and rode off, ringing his bell furiously at a small dog that dared to run across the road in front of him. Was he, the Great Goon, in charge of a First-Class Case, going to wait whilst an old pedlar-woman fished for ages in her petticoats for a licence he didn't really want to see? Gah!

When Goon was safely out of sight the others went back to Fatty, amused and half-alarmed. "Oh, Fatty! How *can* you act like that with Goon? If only he'd known it was really you!"

"I enjoyed that," said Fatty. "Good thing Goon didn't wait to see my licence though, because I haven't got one, of course. Come on – let's get back home. I'm dying to take off these hot clothes. I've got layers of petticoats on to make me fat and shapeless!"

On the way up the village street they passed the bench where they had spoken to the old man on their way to the Fair that afternoon. Bets pointed him out to Fatty.

"Fatty. Do you see that old fellow, sleeping on that bench over there? Well, we thought he was *you*! And we went and called him Fatty, and Pip gave him a poke in the ribs!"

Fatty stood and looked at the old chap. "You know, it would be quite easy to disguise myself like him," he said. "I've a good mind to try it. Honestly, I believe I could."

"But you couldn't make your ears like his," said Bets. "He's got awful ears."

"No, I couldn't. But I could pull my cap down lower than he does, and hide my ears a bit," said Fatty. "Yes, that would be a very good and easy disguise indeed. I'll try it one day. Did Pip really poke him in the ribs?"

"Yes. And the old fellow kept on saying, 'Wassat? Wassat?' " said Pip, with a giggle. "He's deaf, poor old thing."

The old man suddenly opened his eyes and saw the children looking at him. He thought they must have spoken to him. He cupped one of his ears in his hand and croaked out his favourite word, "Wassat?"

The old Balloon-woman winked at the children and sat down beside the old fellow. "Fine evening," she said, in the cracked voice the children were beginning to know well.

"Wassat?" said the old man. Then he sniffed, and

wiped his nose deftly with the back of his hand. Fatty did exactly the same, which made Bets giggle in delight.

"FINE EVENING," said Fatty. "AND A FINE MORNING TOO!"

"Don't know nothing about mornings," said the old man surprisingly. "Always sleep till midday, I do. Then I gets up, has my bit of dinner, and comes out into the sun. Mornings don't mean nothing to me."

He sniffed again, and then took out his pipe to fill it. Fatty watched all he did. Yes, it would be a marvellous thing to do, to disguise himself as this old fellow. Pipe, sniffs, deafness, and all – Fatty could do it!"

"Come on, Fatty!" said Pip, in a low voice. "We really will have to get back. It's getting late."

Fatty got up and joined them. They soon parted and went their different way – Pip and Bets down their lane, and Larry and Daisy up theirs. Fatty went in at his back gate, and his mother caught sight of the old Balloon-woman, as she stood in the garden, cutting sweet-peas for the table.

"A friend of Cook's, I suppose," she thought; "or is she trying to sell balloons here?"

She waited for the Balloon-woman to come back again, but she didn't. So, rather curious, Mrs. Trotteville went to the kitchen door and looked in. There was no Balloon-woman to be seen – only Cook, red in the face, cooking the dinner.

"Where did that old Balloon-woman go?" said Mrs. Trotteville, in wonder. But Cook didn't know. She hadn't seen any old woman at all. And no wonder – for at that moment the old Balloon-woman was stripping off layers of petticoats down in the shed at the bottom of the garden – to come forth as a very hot and rather untidy Fatty.

"What a peculiar thing for a Balloon-woman to vanish into thin air!" thought Mrs. Trotteville. And so it was.

A Visit to Inspector Jenks

Fatty had much enjoyed his fun as the old Balloon-woman, and so had the others. He gave Bets the silver propelling-pencil and she was really delighted.

"I've never had such a lovely pencil," she said. "It writes in red and blue, as well as in ordinary lead. Thank you awfully, Fatty."

"The holidays are going too fast," said Pip, rather gloomily. "And we still haven't got a mystery to solve, though we know that Goon has."

"Yes, I know," said Fatty, looking worried. "I can't bear to think of Goon getting busy on his mystery, and we haven't the least idea what it is. Though it *may* be all those burglaries that are cropping up all over the place, you know – I expect most of the police are keeping their eyes skinned for the gang that is operating such big thefts."

"Can't we keep our eyes skinned too?" said Bets eagerly. "We might see the gang somewhere."

"Idiot! Do you suppose they go about in a crowd together, all looking like burglars?" said Pip scornfully. "They're too jolly clever. They have their own meeting-places their own way of passing on messages, their own ways of disposing of the jewels they steal – haven't they, Fatty? And they are not ways *we* would be likely to find out, even if we did keep our eyes skinned!"

"Oh," said Bets, disappointed. "Well – can't we ask Inspector Jenks if there really *is* a mystery here, and ask him to let us help?"

"Yes – why can't we?" said Daisy. "I'm sure he'd tell us. We've helped him such a lot before."

Inspector Jenks was their very good friend. He was what Bets called "a very high-up policeman," and he belonged to the next big town. In the four mysteries the children had solved before, Inspector Jenks had come in at the end, and been very pleased indeed at all the children had found out. Mr. Goon, however, had not been so pleased, because it was most annoying to him to have those "interfering children messing about with the Law" – especially when they had actually found out things he hadn't.

"I think it's a very good idea of Bets," said Fatty. "Very good indeed. If he knows what the mystery is that Goon is working on – and he's sure to – I don't see why he can't tell us. He knows we'll keep out mouths shut and do all we can to help."

So the next day the Five Find-Outers, with Buster in Fatty's basket, rode on their bicycles to the next big town, where Inspector Jenks had his headquarters. They went to the police-station there, and asked if they might see him.

"What! See the Inspector himself!" said the policeman in charge. "Kids like you! I should think not. He's a Big Man, he is, too busy to bother with kids. Sauce, I call it!"

"Wait a bit," said another policeman, with a nice face,

and very bright blue eyes. "Wait a bit – aren't you the kids that helped with one or two difficult cases over in Peterswood?"

"Yes, we are," said Fatty. "We wouldn't want to bother the Inspector if he's busy, of course – but we would like to ask him something rather important. Important to us, I mean."

"Shall I go in and tell the Inspector then?" said the first policeman to the other one. "Don't want my head bitten off, you know, for interrupting without due cause."

"*I'll* tell him!" said the blue-eyed policeman. "I've heard him talk about these kids." He got up and went out of the room. The children waited as patiently as they could. Surely their old friend would see them!

The policeman came back. "He'll see you," he said. "Come on in."

The children followed him down a long stone-floored passage, and then down another. Bets looked about her half-fearfully. Was she anywhere near prisoners in their cells? She hoped not.

The policeman opened a door with a glass top to it, and announced them. "The children from Peterswood, sir."

The Inspector was sitting at an enormous desk, piled with papers. He was in uniform and looked very big and grand. His eyes twinkled, and he smiled his nice smile.

"Well, well, well!" he said. "The whole lot of you at once – and Buster too, I see! Well, how are you? Come to tell me you've solved the mystery that's been worrying us for months, I suppose!"

He shook hands with them all, and put Bets on his

43

knee. She beamed at him. She was very fond of this big High-Up Policeman.

"No, sir, we haven't come to tell you we've solved any mystery, unfortunately," said Fatty. "These are the first hols for ages that we haven't had a mystery to solve. But sir, we know that Mr. Goon has got one he's working on, and we thought perhaps we could work on it too. But we don't know what it is."

"Yes, Goon's on it," said the Inspector. "In fact, most of the police force of the country seem to be on it too! But it's not one that you can be mixed up in. I don't think you could help at all, first-rate detectives though you are!"

"Oh!" said Fatty, disappointed. "Is it – is it all these big burglaries, sir?"

"Yes, that's right," said the Inspector. "Very clever, they are. The thieves know just what jewels to steal, when to get at them, and lay their plans very carefully. And we don't know one single one of the men! Not one. Though we have our suspicions, you know! We always have!"

He twinkled at the listening children. Fatty felt desperate. Surely the Inspector could tell them more than that. Surely Goon knew more? Else why was he so busy and important these days?

"Mr. Goon looks as if he knew quite a lot, sir," said Fatty. "Is there anything going on in Peterswood at all?"

The Inspector hesitated. "Well," he said at last, "as I said, this is not a thing for children to be mixed up in. Definitely not, and I am sure you would agree with me if you knew what I know. Peterswood is not exactly mixed up in it – but we suspect that some of the gang go there – to meet perhaps – or to pass on messages – we don't know."

The children's eyes brightened immediately. "Sir!" said Fatty, at once, "can't we just keep our eyes open, then? Not snoop round too much, if you don't want us to – but watch and see if we hear or spot anything unusual. Children can often see and hear things that grown-ups can't, because people suspect other grown-ups, but they don't notice children much."

The Inspector tapped with his pencil on his desk. Fatty knew that he was weighing up whether or not to let them keep a watch on things in Peterswood, and his heart beat anxiously. How he hoped they would be allowed just to have a little hand in this Mystery! It seemed a pretty hopeless one, and Mr. Goon was sure to do better than they could, because he knew so much more – but Fatty simply couldn't *bear* to be left out of it altogether!

"All right," said the Inspector at last, and put his pencil down. "You can keep your eyes open for me – but don't plunge headlong into anything foolish or dangerous. Just keep your eyes open. It's barely possible you children might spot something, simply *because* you're children. Report to me if you find anything suspicious."

"Oh, *thank* you!" said every one at once, delighted.

"It's jolly good of you, sir," said Fatty. "We will find out something! And we'll be as careful as Mr. Goon!"

"Well, I'm afraid he will come out on top this time," said the Inspector, his eyes twinkling. "He knows so much more than you do. But I can tell you no more than I have done. Good-bye – and it's been so nice to see you!"

The children went. They got on their bicycles and rode back home, thrilled and pleased. They all went to Pip's garden, and sat down importantly in his summerhouse, right at the top of the garden.

"Well – we've got a Mystery after all!" said Fatty. "Who are the gang that steals all these jewels? Goon's on the job, and he's got a flying start – and now we'll be on it too. Has anybody noticed anything suspicious in Peterswood lately?"

They all thought hard. But nobody could think of anything in the least suspicious. Things seemed to be pretty much as usual, except that the hot weather had brought crowds of people into the little riverside village.

"I can't think of a thing," said Larry.

"It's not a very *easy* Mystery," said Daisy, frowning. "There doesn't seem anywhere to begin."

"Can't we do it the usual way – find clues, and make a list of Suspects?" said Bets.

"Right!" said Pip scornfully. "You tell us what clues to look for, and who to put down on a list of Suspects!"

"There are no clues to look for, and we don't even know where to look for Suspects," said Larry mournfully. "I wonder what Goon knows."

"He's probably got a list of men he's suspicious of," said Fatty thoughtfully. "And he's also probably got all details of all the burglaries committed lately. I'd better get some back numbers of the newspapers and read them up. Not that it will help us very much, really."

There was a long pause. "Well," said Pip, at last, "What's the plan? What are we going to do?"

There simply didn't seem *anything* to do! All they

knew was that it was possible that the thieves some-times met in Peterswood.

"I think it wouldn't be a bad idea for me to disguise myself as that old deaf fellow, who sits on that sunny bench in the middle of the village," said Fatty. "We know he isn't there in the mornings, so that would be the time for me to go and sit there. I might be able to spot something suspicious. Men passing notes to one another as they meet – or making remarks in low voices – or even sitting on that bench and talking."

Every one looked doubtful. It didn't seem at all likely, really. Bets guessed that Fatty wanted the fun of disguising himself again. "You had certainly better not be there in the afternoon!" she said. "People would begin to wonder, if they saw *two* old fellows, exactly alike, sitting on the same bench!"

"Yes. Goon would have a fit!" said Larry, and every one laughed.

"Don't you think it would be better if you chose some other disguise, not disguise yourself like that old fel-low?" said Pip. "Just in case you did both wander along at the same time? There doesn't really seem any point in dressing up like that dirty old man."

"There isn't, really. I just feel I'd like to, that's all," said Fatty. "You know, if you're as good an actor as I am, there are certain parts or characters that appeal to you much more than others. I loved being that old Balloon-woman – and I shall love to be that old man. I can act him exactly right."

He gave a realistic sniff and wiped his nose with the back of his hand. The others laughed, and did not tease him over his boasting of being such a good actor.

"You're disgusting!" said Daisy. "Don't for goodness

sake start doing that sort of thing in front of your parents! They'll have a fit!"

Fatty got up and hobbled out into the garden, shuffling like the old man. He bent his back and dropped his head. He really was an extremely good actor.

Then he gave another frightful sniff and wiped his nose on his sleeve.

A horrified voice spoke to him. "Frederick! Haven't you a handkerchief? What disgusting behaviour!"

And there was Pip's mother, come to fetch them in to a meal, as they all seemed completely deaf to the gong. Poor Fatty! He went red to the ears, and produced an enormous handkerchief at once. How the others laughed!

Something Rather Queer

With the help of the others, Fatty managed to get together some old clothes very like the old man on the bench had worn. Pip produced a very old gardening hat belonging to his father. Larry found an old coat hanging in the garage.

"It's been there for years, as far as I remember," he said. "Nobody ever wears it. You might as well have it. It's got mildew inside the pockets, so be careful how you put your hands in them!"

It was easy to get an old shirt and muffler. Fatty produced a torn shirt of his own, and found a muffler down in the garden shed, which he must have left there months before.

He dragged the shirt in the dirt, and it was soon as filthy as the old man's. He dirtied the muffler a little more too.

"What about the shoes?" he said. "We want frightfully old ones. That old man's were all cracked open at the toe."

The shoes were a real problem. Noboby's father had shoes as old as that. The children wondered if they could buy a pair from some tramp, but when they went out to find a tramp, the only one they met had perfectly good shoes on.

Then Daisy had a brain-wave. "Let's look in all the ditches we pass!" she said. "There are always old boots and shoes in ditches, I don't know why. We might find some there."

Sure enough they did! Larry came across a dirty, damp old pair, open at the toes and well worn at the heels. He tossed them to Fatty.

"Well, if you think you really do want to wear such horrible things, there you are! But you'll have to dry them or you'll get awfully damp feet, and have a streaming cold."

"He'll be able to sniffle properly then," said Bets. She too had been practising the old man's sniff, much to her mother's annoyance.

"I'll put them under the tank in the hot cupboard," said Fatty. "They'll soon dry there. They'll about fit me. I don't at all like wearing them, but, after all, if it's important to solve the Mystery, it's important to put up with little things like this!"

The trousers seemed quite impossible to get. Nobody's father wore the kind of coarse corduroy that the old man wore. Could they possibly buy a pair in

"*Just what we want,*" said Fatty

the village shop and make them torn and dirty for Fatty to wear?

"Better not buy them in Peterswood, in case the news gets round," said Fatty. "I wouldn't want old Goon to know I'd bought workman's corduroys – he'd be sure to snoop round and find out why. He's got more brains lately, somehow."

"We'll walk across the fields to Sheepridge," said Daisy. "We might buy a pair there."

Half-way across the fields Pip gave a shout that made every one jump. He pointed to an old scarecrow standing forgotten in a field. It wore a hat without a brim, a ragged coat – and a pair of dreadful old corduroy trousers!

"Just what we want!" said Fatty joyfully, and ran to the scarecrow. "We'll give them back to him when we've finished with them. Golly, aren't they holey? I hope they'll hang together on me."

"I'd better give them a wash for you," said Daisy. "They really are awful. If you wear your pair of brown flannel shorts under them, Fatty, the holes won't show up so much. There are really too many to mend."

Joyfully the Find-Outers went back to Larry's. Daisy washed the trousers, but not much dirt came out of them because the rain had washed them many a time. Bets couldn't imagine how Fatty could bear to put on such horrid old clothes.

"Duty calls!" said Fatty, with a grin. "Got to do all kinds of unpleasant things, Bets, when duty calls. And a really good detective doesn't stick at anything."

The next day they held a dress rehearsal and dressed Fatty up in the old clothes. He had already got a ragged, sandy-grey beard, which he had cut more or less to the shape of the old man's. He had shaggy grey eyebrows to put on too, and wisps of straggly grey hair to peep out from under his hat.

He made himself up carefully. He put in some wrinkles with his grease-paints, and then screwed up his mouth so that it looked as if he hadn't many teeth.

"Oh, Fatty – you're marvellous!" cried Bets. "I simply can't bear to look at you, you look so awful. Don't stare at me like that! You give me the creeps! You're an old, old man, not Fatty at all!"

"Wassat?" said Fatty, putting his hand behind his ear. He had very dirty hands indeed – and this tme he had remembered to blacken his nails too. He really looked appalling.

"What's the time?" he asked, for he had taken off his wrist-watch, in case it showed. "Oh, twelve o'clock. Well, what about shuffling off for a snooze in the sun, on that bench? My double won't be there, because he said he never goes out till the afternoon. Come on. I'll see if I can play my part all right!"

"We'll all come," said Pip. "But we'll not sit near you. We'll go and have lemonade in that little sweet-shop opposite the bench. We can keep an eye on you then, and see what happens."

Fatty, after sending Larry down his garden path to the back gate, to see if the coast was clear, shuffled down, hoping that nobody in his house would spot him. He didn't want his mother to get curious about the odd old men and women that seemed to haunt her back-entrance.

Once out in the road, the other four children kept near to Fatty, but not near enough to make any one suspect they were with him. He shuffled along, dragging his feet, bent and stooping, his hat well down over his ears.

"He's just *exactly* like that old fellow we saw!" whispered Bets to Daisy. "I'd never know the difference, would you?"

Fatty did a loud sniff and the others grinned. He came to the sunny bench and cautiously sat himself down, giving a little sigh as he did so. "Aaaah!"

He was certainly a marvellous actor. He sat there in the sun, bending over his stick, the very picture of a poor old man having a rest. The others made their way to the little lemonade shop, and sat down at the table in the window to watch him.

Just as they were finishing their lemonade a man came by on a bicycle, whistling. He was a perfectly ordinary man, in a perfectly ordinary suit and cap, with a very ordinary face. But, when he caught sight of the old man, he braked very suddenly indeed, and looked at him in some astonishment.

He got off his bicycle and wheeled it over to the bench. He leaned it against the seat and sat down by Fatty. The children, watching from the shop opposite, were surprised and rather alarmed. Had this man seen something queer about Fatty's disguise? Had he guessed it was somebody pretending? Would he give Fatty away?

Fatty, too, felt a little alarmed. He had been enjoying himself thoroughly, getting right "under the skin" of the old man, as he put it to himself. He had seen the look of surprise on the man's face. Now here he was sitting beside him. Why?

"What you out here for, in the morning?" said the man suddenly, in a very low voice. "Thought you never

53

came till the afternoon. Anything up? Expecting any one?"

Fatty was taken aback to hear this low and confidential whisper. Obviously the man thought him to be the old fellow, and was amazed to see him out in the morning. But what did all the questions mean?

Just in time, Fatty remembered that the old man was deaf. He put his hand to his ear and put his ear towards the man, so that he should not look directly into his face. He was afraid that he might be recognized as a fraud if the man looked into his eyes.

"Wassat?" said Fatty, in a croaking old voice. "Wassat?"

The man gave an impatient exclamation. "Of course – he's deaf!" He gave a quick look round as if to see if any one was near. Then somebody else cycled slowly by and the man sidled a little way away from Fatty, and took out a cigarette to light.

The cyclist was Goon, perspiring freely in the hot sun. He saw the two men at once, and got off his bicycle. He pretended to adjust the chain. The four children in the shop watched him with interest, hoping that he wouldn't go and say anything to Fatty.

Buster saw Goon, and with a delighted yelp he tore out of the sweet-shop, and danced round the policeman's feet. Larry rushed after him, afraid that Buster would go and lick Fatty's face, and give the show away to Goon. But Buster was fully engaged with the angry policeman, and was having a perfectly lovely time, dodging kicks, and getting in little snaps and snarls whenever he could.

Fatty got up hurriedly and shuffled away round the nearest corner without being noticed by Mr. Goon, who was rapidly losing his temper. All the others, seeing that Fatty wanted to get away before Goon noticed he was gone, began to join in the fun, pretending to call Buster off, but only succeeding in exciting the little Scottie more than ever!

When at last Buster was safely in Larry's arms, and Goon could look round at the bench, it was empty! Both the men had gone. Mr. Goon looked extremely angry.

"That there dog!" he said, dusting his trousers down violently. "I'll report him, I will. Interfering with me doing my duty, that's what he did. And now where are them two fellows gone? I wanted to put a few questions to them!"

"They've disappeared," said Daisy. Mr. Goon did one of his snorts.

"No need to tell me that. I've got eyes in my head, haven't I? I may have lost a Most Important Clue! See? Where's that fat boy that's always with you? I bet he's at the bottom of this!"

"He isn't here," said Larry truthfully. "You'll probably find him at home if you badly want to see him, Mr. Goon."

"I wouldn't care if I never set eyes on him again, the cheeky toad!" said Mr. Goon, mounting his bicycle rather ponderishly and wobbling a little. "No, nor any of you neither. As for that dog!"

He was about to ride off, when he stopped, wobbled again, and spoke to Larry.

"Where were you just now?"

"In the sweet-shop, having lemonade," said Larry.

"Ho," said Mr. Goon. "And did you see that old fellow sitting on that bench?"

"Yes, we did," said Larry. "He seemed half-asleep and quite harmless."

"And did you see that other fellow talking to him?" demanded Mr. Goon.

"Well – he may have spoken to him. I don't know," said Larry, wondering why the policeman was asking all these questions.

"You'd better come alonga me," said Mr. Goon, at last. "I'm going to call on that old fellow, see, and I want you to back me up when I tell him I want to know about the other fellow."

The children felt distinctly alarmed. What! Mr. Goon was going to visit the *real* old man – who would probably be in bed – and ask him questions about the other man, whom he hadn't been there to see! Whatever would the poor old fellow say? He wouldn't in the least know what Mr. Goon was talking about!

The First Clue

"I don't think we've got time to ..." began Larry. But Mr. Goon pooh-poohed him.

"It's my orders," he said pompously. "You may be witnesses. You come alonga me."

So the children went with Mr. Goon, Buster struggling wildly against the lead to get at the policeman's ankles. They turned one or two corners and came to a dirty little pair of cottages at one end of a lane. Mr. Goon went to the first one and knocked.

There was no answer at all. He knocked again. The children felt uncomfortable and wished they were at home. No answer. Then Mr. Goon pushed hard at the door and it opened into a room that was plainly half sitting-room and half bedroom. It was very dirty and smelt horrid.

In the far corner was a small bed, piled high with dirty bedclothes. In it, apparently asleep, his grey hairs showing above the blanket, was the old man. His clothes were on a chair beside him – old coat, corduroy trousers, shirt, muffler, hat, and shoes.

"Hey, you!" said Mr. Goon, marching in. "No good pretending to be asleep, see? I saw you a few minutes ago in the village street, on the bench."

The old man awoke with a jump. He seemed to be extremely surprised to see Mr. Goon in his room. He sat up and stared at him. "Wassat?" he said. It really did seem to be about the only thing he could say.

"It's no good pretending to be in bed and asleep," roared Mr. Goon. "You were on the bench in the middle of the street just now. I saw you!"

"I ain't been out of this room today!" said the old man, in a cracked voice. "I always sleeps till dinner, I do."

"You don't," shouted Mr. Goon. "You didn't today. And I want to know what that fellow said to you when he came and sat beside you on the bench. Now you tell me, or it'll be the worse for you!"

Bets felt sorry for the old man. She hated it when Mr. Goon shouted so. The old fellow looked more and more puzzled.

"Wassat?" he said, going back to the word he loved.

"See these children here?" said Mr. Goon, beside himself with annoyance at the old man's stupidity. "Well, they saw you there too. Speak up now, you kids.

You saw him, didn't you?"

"Well," said Larry, hesitating. "Well ..." He really didn't know what to say. He knew quite well it hadn't been the old man on the bench – and yet how could he say so without giving Fatty away?

Pip saw his difficulty and rushed in with a few clever words. "You see, Mr. Goon, it's difficult to say, isn't it, because an old man in bed and an old man dressed don't look a bit the same."

"Well, look at his clothes then," said Mr. Goon, pointing to the clothes. "Aren't those the very clothes he was dressed in?"

"They might not be," said Pip. "Sorry, Mr. Goon, but we can't help you in the matter."

Larry thought it was about time to go, for Mr. Goon's face was turning a familiar purple. So he and the others hurriedly went back up the lane and made their way to Fatty's, longing to tell him all that had happened.

They found Fatty in the wood-shed at the bottom of his garden, trying to make himself a bit respectable. All his old-man clothes were in a sack, ready for use again. He was just smoothing down his hair when the others poured in.

"I say!" began Fatty, his eyes bright. "That was a bit queer, wasn't it? I mean – that man being so surprised to see me – and sitting down and saying things to me. I almost forgot I was deaf and shouldn't hear them!"

"What did he say?" asked Pip, and Fatty told him. The others listened breathlessly.

"And then up comes Goon, spots this fellow, and makes an awful to-do about adjusting his bike-chain, in order to have a good squint at the chap," said Larry.

"Looks suspicious to me. I mean – it looks as if Goon knew the fellow and wanted to know what he was up to."

"Is it a clue?" asked Bets eagerly.

"You and your clues!" said Pip scornfully. "Don't be silly, Bets."

"I don't think she *is* silly," said Fatty thoughtfully. "I think it *is* a clue – a clue to something that's going on – maybe even something to do with the Mystery. You know what the Inspector said – that it is thought that Peterswood may be the meeting-place of the thief-gang – the place where messages are passed on, perhaps, from one member to another."

"And perhaps the old man is the fellow who takes the messages and passes them on!" cried Daisy. "Oh, Fatty! Is he the chief burglar, do you think?"

"Course not," said Fatty. "Can you imagine a poor feeble old thing like that doing anything violent? No, he's just a convenient message-bearer, I should think. Nobody would ever suspect him, sitting out there in the sun, half-asleep. It would be easy enough for any one to go and whisper anything to him."

"But he's deaf," objected Daisy.

"So he is. Well then, maybe they slip him messages," said Fatty. "Golly – I feel we're on to something!"

"Let's think," said Larry. "We shall get somewhere, I feel, if we think!"

They all thought. Bets was so excited that not a single sensible thought came into her head. It was Fatty as usual who came out with everything clear and simple.

"I've got it!" he said. "Probably Peterswood *is* the headquarters of the gang, for some reason or other, and when one member wants to get into touch with another, they don't communicate with each other directly, which would be dangerous, but send messages by that old fellow. And, Find-Outers, if I go and sit on that bench day in and day out, I've no doubt some of the members of the gang will come along, sit by me, and deliver messages in some way, and . . ."

"And you'll learn who they are, and we can tell the Inspector, and he'll have them arrested!" cried Bets, in great excitement.

"Well, something like that," said Fatty. "The thing is – the old man always sits there in the afternoon, and that's really when I ought to sit there, because it's then that any messages will come. But how can I sit there, if *he's* there?"

"That's why that man was so surprised this morning," said Daisy. "He knew the old man never *was* there in the mornings – and yet it seemed as if he was, this morning! He never guessed it was you. Your disguise must have been perfect."

"It must have been," said Fatty modestly. "The thing is – can we possibly stop the old fellow from going there in the afternoons? If we could, I could sit on that bench, and you could all sit in the sweet-shop and watch."

"We can't drink lemonade for hours," said Bets.

"You could take it in turn," said Fatty. "The thing is, we *must* take notice of what the messengers are like, so that we should recognize them again. I shan't dare to look at them too closely, in case they suspect something. So you would have to notice very carefully indeed. I shall take whatever messages they pass on to me, and leave it to you to see exactly what the men are

60

like that come to see me on that bench."

"What about that one this morning?" said Larry suddenly. "That must have been one of them. Now – what exactly was he like?"

Every one frowned and tried to remember. "He was simply too ordinary for anything," said Larry at last. "Ordinary face, ordinary clothes, ordinary bicycle. Wait though – I'm remembering something about that bicycle. It had a – it had a hooter on it, instead of a bell!"

"So it had!" said Pip, remembering too. Daisy and Bets hadn't noticed that. In fact, they couldn't remember a thing about the man at all.

"A hooter," said Fatty thoughtfully. "Well, that might be a bit of help in tracing the man. We'll keep a lookout for bikes with hooters. But the thing that's really worrying me *is* – how can we stop that old man from sitting on the bench in the afternoons, so that *I* can go instead?"

Nobody knew. "The only thing is," said Fatty at last, "the absolutely only thing is – for me to slide down on the bench beside him, and pretend to be one of the messengers myself – and tell him not to sit out there for two or three days!"

"Ooooh yes!" said Pip. "Because Mr. Goon may be watching. You could say that."

"I could. And it will probably be quite true," said Fatty, with a groan. "Old Goon has got his suspicions too, and is on the right track. We've tumbled on it by accident. There I shall sit, under Goon's eye all the afternoon! bet no messenger will come if they know that he's watching."

"If we see a likely-looking stranger hanging about, we could get Goon away for a bit," said Larry. "And I know how we could do it too! We could go round a corner and toot a hooter! Then Goon would think to himself, 'Ha, hooter on a bike! Maybe the man I want!' and go scooting round the corner."

"Yes, that's quite well worked out," said Fatty. "The thing is – Goon probably hasn't noticed the hooter on the man's bike."

"Well, tell him then," said Larry. "He'll be awfully bucked at that. Let's go and tell him now."

"Come on then. We'll go and look for him," said Fatty. But just then Larry looked at his watch and gave an exclamation. "Golly! We'll be *fright*fully late for lunch! We'll have to tell Goon this afternoon."

"I will," said Fatty. "See you later!"

That afternoon Mr. Goon, enjoying a brief afternoon dinner nap, was surprised to see Fatty coming in at the door, and even more surprised when the boy presented his bit of information about the hooter on the bicycle.

"I don't know if it will be of any use to you, Mr. Goon," he said, earnestly. "But we thought you ought to know. After all, it's a clue, isn't it?"

"Ho! A clue to what?" demanded Mr. Goon. "You aren't interfering again, are you? And anyway, I noticed that there hooter myself. And if I hear it tooting, I'll soon be after the cyclist."

"What do you want him for?" asked Fatty innocently.

Mr. Goon stared at him suspiciously. "Never you mind. And look here, how is it you know all about this here hooter, when you wasn't with the others? You tell me that."

"Oh, *they* told me," said Fatty. "I'm afraid you're angry with me for trying to give you a clue, Mr. Goon.

I'm sorry. I didn't know you had already noticed the hooter. I won't trouble you with any of our information again."

"Now look here, there's no harm in ..." began Mr. Goon, afraid that perhaps Fatty might withhold further information that might really be of use. But Fatty was gone. He visited a shop on the way home and bought a very nice little rubber hooter. Mr. Goon was going to hear it quite a lot! In fact, he heard it a few minutes later, just outside his window, as he was finishing his nap. He shot upright at once, and raced to the door.

But there was no cyclist to be seen. He went back slowly – and the hooter sounded again. Drat it! Where was it? He looked up and down the road once more but there really was no sign of a bicycle. There was only a boy a good way down, sauntering along. But he hadn't a bicycle.

He had a hooter, though, under his coat, and his name was Fatty!

Fatty Delivers His Message

The next afternoon Fatty did not dress up as the old man, but instead, put on his Balloon-woman's petticoats and shawls again. The others watched him, down in the shed at the bottom of Fatty's garden. Bets thought she could watch him for days on end, making himself up as different people. There was no doubt at all that Fatty had a perfect gift for dressing up and acting.

"I'll go and sit on the seat beside the old man," said

Fatty. "He's sure to be there this afternoon, waiting for any possible messages – and you can snoop round and see if Goon is anywhere about. If he isn't, I'll take the chance of telling the old man not to appear for a few afternoons as the police are watching. That should make him scuttle away all right if he's in with the gang!"

"I'll come and buy another balloon from you," said Bets eagerly. "That will make it all seem real."

"Oh, it'll be real enough," said Fatty. "All I hope is that Goon won't come and ask me for my licence again."

"He won't, if you are sitting in the middle of the village street, and he thinks you've got to hunt all through your petticoats for it, and make him look silly," said Larry. "He can't bear to be made to look silly. And anyway, he won't want to draw attention to himself if he's watching for any possible gang members. He won't think *you're* one."

"Quite right," said Fatty. "Well reasoned out, Larry. Now – am I ready?"

"You look simply marvellous," said Bets admiringly. "You really do. I can't think how you manage to make your face go so different, Fatty. It doesn't look a bit like you."

"Oh, I practise in front of a mirror," said Fatty. "And I've got some marvellous books about it. And, of course, I've got the *gift* – you see . . ."

"Oh, shut up, Fatty," said Larry good humouredly. "We all know you're marvellous, without *you* telling us!"

The Balloon-woman suddenly screwed up her face, and her mouth went down at the corners in a most pathetic manner. She fished out a big red handkerchief, decidedly dirty, and began to weep most realistically.

"Don't be so unkind to me," she wept, and the others roared with laughter. Fatty peeped out at them from the corner of his hanky. "A pore old woman like me!" he wept. "Sleeping out under hedges at night . . ."

"With layers of petticoats to keep you warm!" chuckled Larry. Then he stopped and looked quickly out of the window of the shed.

"Quick! There's your mother, Fatty. What shall we do?"

There wasn't time to do anything. Mrs. Trotteville was even then looking in at the door. She had come to speak to the children, but when she saw the old Balloon-woman, she was very much astonished.

"What are you doing here?" she asked sharply. "I saw you going down the garden-path the other day."

Bets spoke up before Fatty could answer.

"She sells lovely balloons," she said. "I want to buy one, Mrs. Trotteville."

"There's absolutely no need to buy one in the garden-shed," said Mrs. Trotteville. "You can buy one in the street. I don't want pedlars or tramps in the garden. I am surprised that Buster did not bark."

Buster was there, of course, sitting at the Balloon-woman's feet. He looked as if she was his best friend — as indeed she was, if only Mrs. Trotteville had known it.

"Where's Frederick?" asked Mrs. Trotteville, looking all round for Fatty.

"Er – not far away," said Larry truthfully. "Er – shall I go and look for him, Mrs. Trotteville?"

"Oh no. I suppose you are all waiting for him," said

Mrs. Trotteville. "Well, I'm afraid this woman and her balloons must go – and please do not come into the garden again!"

"No, Mum," said the Balloon-woman, and bobbed a funny little curtsey that nearly sent Bets into fits of laughter. They all went out of the shed and up the path to the front gate.

"That was a narrow squeak," said Larry, when they were safely out in the road.

"Narrow squeaks are exciting!" said Pip.

They made their way to the main street of the village. There, on the sunny bench, was the old man as usual, bent over his stick, looking half-asleep.

"I'll go and sit down by him," said Fatty, swinging his voluminous skirts out around him as he walked. "You walk behind me now, and keep a watch out for Goon. Bets can tell me if he's anywhere about when she comes to buy a balloon. You can all go and have lemonade in that shop, to begin with."

The Balloon-woman sat down on the bench with her bunch of gay balloons. The old man at the end of the seat took no notice of her at all. The balloons bobbed in the wind, and passers-by looked at them with pleasure. A mother stopped to buy one for her baby, and the four watching children giggled as they saw Fatty bend over the baby in the pram and tickle its cheek.

"How does he know how to do things like that?" chuckled Larry. "I'd never think of those things."

"But it's those little touches that make his disguises so real," said Daisy, in admiration. They went into the lemonade shop and sat down to have a drink. A man was sitting at a table nearby, lost in a big newspaper. Larry glanced at him, and then gave Pip a kick under the table. Pip looked up and Larry winked at him, and nodded his head slightly towards the man.

The others looked – and there was old Clear-Orf, in plain clothes, pretending to read a newspaper, and keeping an eye on the bench across the road, just as they too intended to do!

"Good morning, Mr. Goon," said Larry politely. "Having a day off?"

Mr. Goon grunted bad-temperedly. Those children again! They seemed to turn up everywhere.

"You having a lemonade too?" said Pip. "Have one with us, Mr. Goon. Do."

Mr. Goon grunted again, and returned to his newspaper. He was in plain clothes and looked rather strange. The children couldn't remember ever having seen him in anything but his rather tight-fitting uniform before. He wore flannel trousers, a cream shirt open at the neck, and a belt that he had pulled too tight. Bets thought he didn't look like Mr. Goon at all.

She finished her lemonade. "I'm going to buy a balloon," she said. "The one I bought at the Fair has gone pop. Order me an ice, Pip, and I'll be back to have it soon. We *are* all going to have ices, aren't we?"

"Where's that fat boy?" asked Mr. Goon, as Bets got up.

"Fat boy? What fat boy?" said Larry at once, pretending to be puzzled.

Mr. Goon gave a snort. "That boy Frederick. Fatty, you call him. You know quite well who I mean. Don't act so daft."

"Oh, *Fatty*! He's not far off," said Larry. "Do you want to see him? I'll tell him, if you like."

"*I* don't want to see him," said Mr. Goon. "But I

67

know he's always up to something. What's he up to now?"

"*Is* he up to something now?" said Larry, a surprised look on his face. "How mean of him not to tell us!"

Bets giggled and went out. She crossed the road to where the old Balloon-woman sat, her skirts almost filling half of the bench.

"May I have a blue balloon, please?" she said. She bent over the bunch of balloons and whispered to Fatty. "Mr. Goon is in the lemonade shop – in plain clothes. He looks so funny. I think he's watching the old man. You'll have to watch till you see Mr. Goon go off, and then give your message."

"Have *this* balloon, little Miss!" said the Balloon-woman, winking at Bets to show that her message had been heard. "This is a fine strong one. Last you for weeks!"

Bets paid for it, and went back to the shop. Larry had just ordered ices. He raised his eyebrows at Bets to ask her if she had delivered the message all right. She nodded. They began to eat their ices slowly, wondering if the policeman meant to stay in the shop all the afternoon.

They had almost finished their ices when the telephone went at the back of the shop. The shop-woman answered it. "For you, please, Mr. Goon," she said.

Mr. Goon got up, went to the dark corner at the back of the shop, and listened to what the telephone had to say. Larry took a look at him. Goon could not possibly see across the street to the bench from where he stood. Now would be Fatty's chance to give his message to the old man!

"It's hot in here," said Larry, suddenly standing up.

"I'm going out for a breath of air. You come when you've finished your ices."

He went out of the shop and shot across to the bench. He sat down beside the Balloon-woman. "Goon's telephoning," he said. "Now's your chance. He can't see across the street from where the telephone is."

"Right," said Fatty. He moved nearer to the old man and nudged him. The old fellow looked round at once. Fatty slipped a note to him and then moved back to his end of the bench.

The old man deftly pocketed the note and sat for a few minutes more. Then, with a grunt, he got up and shuffled off round the corner. Larry followed him, at a sign from Fatty. As soon as he was safely round the corner the old fellow opened the slip of paper and looked at it. Then he took a match, lighted the paper, and let it drop to the ground, where it burnt away.

He did not go back to his bench. Instead, he shuffled off in the direction of his home. Larry went back to the bench and stood beside the old Balloon-woman, pretending to choose a balloon.

"Did he read the note?" said Fatty, in a low voice.

"Yes. And he's gone off home now, I think," said Larry. "What did you put in the note?"

"I just put that he'd better not come to this seat for three afternoons as the police were watching it," said Fatty. "He'll think it was from a member of the gang, I expect. He will think they'd asked me to pass the message to him, as they wouldn't want to be seen doing it themselves, if the seat was watched. Well, let's hope we've got him out of the way for a few days!"

"I'll have this balloon," said Larry, as some people passed. "How much?"

Taking the balloon with him, he went back to the door of the shop. Mr. Goon was still telephoning. Good! The others got up and went out. They all sauntered down the road, thinking how cross Mr. Goon would be when he stopped telephoning and found that the old man was gone.

The Balloon-woman went too. It had been decided that she should go to Pip's garden, in case Mrs. Trotteville, Fatty's mother, should spot her again, going down her garden-path, and make trouble. Pip's mother was out for the day, so it would be safe for Fatty to go there and change back to himself.

Soon all the Find-Outers, and Buster, were in Pip's summer-house. Fatty changed as quickly as he could.

"I shan't use this disguise more than I can help," he said, pushing all the petticoats and skirts into the sack he kept them in. "It's too hot. I shall get as thin as a rake if I keep getting so melting-hot!"

"Oh, don't do that!" said Bets, in alarm. "You wouldn't be Fatty any more, if you were thin. And I do like you just exactly as you are!"

Everybody Does Something

Plans were laid for the next few days. "These may be very important days," said Fatty. "We may be able to learn a lot – right under Goon's nose, too, if he's going to do this watch-dog act of his!"

"What exactly are we going to do?" said Daisy, thrilled. "You're going to disguise yourself as that old man, we know, and take his place, hoping for a message from one of the gang. But what are *we* to do? We must have something interesting so that we can do our share as Find-Outers."

"Woof," said Buster.

"He wants a job too," said Bets, with a laugh. "Poor Buster! He can't understand why you have to dress up as somebody different, Fatty. You don't look or sound the same to him – you only *smell* the same. And when you go out as the Balloon-woman or the old man, we have to lock Buster up and leave him behind, and he hates that."

"Poor old Buster-Dog," said Fatty, and at once Buster rolled himself over on his back to be tickled. His tongue came out, and his tail wagged so violently that it wagged his whole body and made it shake from end to end.

"Now," said Fatty, taking out his note-book and opening it. "Let's just have a look at what we know. Then we'll make our plans – and you shall each have something to do."

"Good," said Larry. "I know you've got to do all the important work, Fatty, because you really are a born detective – but we do want something as well."

"We don't know very much yet," said Fatty, looking at his notes. "We know that Goon is watching the old man because he suspects what we do – that he receives messages to pass on – and we feel certain that for some reason or other the headquarters are here in Peterswood. We have also seen one of the members of the gang – the fellow with a hooter on his bike – but that's about all we *do* know."

"It's not very much," said Larry. "Not a scrap more than we knew the other day."

71

"We also know that the old fellow is likely to keep away from that seat for a while," said Fatty. "Goon doesn't know that. We're ahead of him there. *We* know that the old man who will be sitting on the bench this afternoon, and tomorrow and probably the next day too, will be *me* – and not that old fellow."

"Yes, that's one up to us," said Pip.

"Now," said Fatty, shutting his note-book and looking round, "tomorrow afternoon – in fact, each afternoon that I sit out on that bench, one or more of you must be in that sweet-shop, watching carefully to see if any one gives me a message – and it's your job to notice every single detail about him very carefully indeed. See? That's most important."

"Right," said Larry.

"And the other thing for you Find-Outers to do is to try and discover which cyclists have hooters on their bikes, instead of bells," said Fatty. "It would be a help if we could discover who that man was that came and spoke to me on the bench the other morning. We could watch him, and find out who his friends were, for instance."

"I don't see how we can possibly find out who has a hooter on his bicycle," said Pip. "We can't go and look into every one's bicycle sheds!"

"You could go to the shop that sells hooters and get into talk with the shopkeeper, and ask him if he sells many hooters, and maybe even get him to tell you the names of the buyers," said Fatty.

"Oh yes," said Pip. "I hadn't thought of that."

"I thought of it the other day when I went to buy that hooter," said Fatty. "But I hadn't time to talk to the man then – well, actually it's a boy in the shop I went

72

to. I should think he'd love to have a good old jaw with you."

"I'd like to go and talk to him," said Bets. "With Daisy."

"You and Daisy and Pip can go, if you like," said Larry. "And I'll watch the seat from the sweet-shop. Then, when you come back with all the information you can get you can take your turn at sitting in the shop and having lemonade, and I'll go and try and find out something else."

"Buster can go with the ones who are going to the hooter-shop," said Fatty. "But he mustn't go to the sweet-shop. He would smell me all across the road, and come bounding out, barking. Goon would soon think there was something funny about Buster making up to a dirty old man!"

The next afternoon Larry went out to the sweet-shop opposite the bench, and ordered a lemonade. Mr. Goon was there again, reading his newspaper. He was once more in plain clothes, and he scowled at Larry when he came in.

"Why, Mr. Goon! Here again!" said Larry, pretending to be most surprised. "You *are* having a nice holiday! Do you spend all your time in here?"

Mr. Goon took absolutely no notice. He felt very angry. Here was he, forced to spend his afternoons in a hot, smelly, little shop, watching a bench out there in the sun – and he couldn't even have peace! Those children had got to come and poke fun at him. Mr. Goon eyed Larry's back grimly, and thought of all the things he would like to do to him and the other Find-Outers.

Then Mr. Goon straightened up a little, for the old man was coming shuffling along to his bench. Larry watched him. He knew it was Fatty, of course, but Mr. Goon didn't. Larry marvelled at the way Fatty lowered himself slowly down on to the bench. That was just exactly the way bent old people did sit down! Fatty never made a mistake in his acting.

Fatty took out a pipe and began slowly to fill it. Then he coughed. It was a horrible, hollow cough, and bent him double. Larry grinned. The cough was new. He supposed Fatty must have heard the old man, and had practised the cough till it was quite perfect.

The old man put his pipe away without smoking it. Evidently he was afraid of its making him cough too much! Larry turned to Mr. Goon.

"There's that old man you made us go and see the other day, Mr. Goon. Funny about him, wasn't it? Did you ever find out what you wanted to know?"

Mr. Goon again took no notice, but rustled the paper noisily. Larry winked at the shop-woman. "Must have got a cold," he said sympathetically. "Gone quite deaf!"

"Now, you look 'ere!" said Mr. Goon, going red and rising quite suddenly, "if you don't . . ."

But just then two men came along, stopped by the bench and sat down. At once Mr. Goon subsided, and began to watch the men with much concentration. So did Larry. Were they going to pass a message to Fatty?

The men had papers. They opened them and began to discuss something. One of them lighted a pipe. They stayed there for quite a time, but neither Goon nor Larry could spot any message being given or received. The old fellow at the end of the bench still leaned over his stick, his head nodding occasionally.

Then he sat upright, gave a loud sniff and wiped the back of his hand across his nose. Larry was amused to see the two men give him a disgusted look. They folded their newspapers, got up, and, still talking, walked off down the street.

Mr. Goon leaned back and wrote down a few notes. Larry wondered if he thought they were the members of the gang. He was certain they weren't. For one thing he was sure that one of them was a friend of his father's.

Larry began to be bored. He had finished his lemonade. He really didn't want another, and he felt that he couldn't possibly eat an ice at that moment. The shopwoman came up to him.

"Anything else, sir?" she asked. Larry said no thank you.

"Well, you go, then," said Mr. Goon's voice. "No need for you to hang about here if you've finished your everlasting lemonade, see?"

This was awkward. Larry was supposed to watch the bench and Fatty until the others came back. He couldn't very well leave his post. But just at that moment the others *did* come back! They clattered in, chattering.

Larry stood up at once. "Hallo, you others! I'm glad you've come for me. I suppose Pip wants to stay and have a lemonade as usual. Well, you girls and I will go and leave him guzzling!' "

For a wonder even Bets sensed that Larry wanted to leave only one of them behind. So the girls went off with Larry, and left Pip to seat himself at the window-table, with a glowering Mr. Goon nearby. Was he *never* going to get rid of these children!

Larry took the girls off, and when they were safely round the corner, he told them how Mr. Goon had ordered him to go. "So I thought we'd better only just leave Pip behind," he said, "and then that still leaves

75

two more of us to go in singly and drink lemonade or eat ices. I think Goon is getting suspicious of us!"

"Larry! We had a most interesting time at the shop where the hooters are sold," said Bets. "Listen!"

She told Larry all about it. She and Pip and Daisy had gone into the shop, which sold bicycles, tyres, pumps, bells, hooters, torches, toys, prams, and many other things. There was a cheeky-looking boy in charge.

"Afternoon," he said, when they all trooped in. "And what may I do for *you*? Want a pram, perhaps?"

Bets giggled. "No," she said. "We want a hooter. My bell isn't very good, and I thought a hooter would make quite a change."

"Well, you're lucky," said the boy, going over to a shelf and getting down a rubber hooter. "We only had these in last week. First we've had for months!"

The children tried it. It hooted very nicely indeed. Parp-parp! Parp-parp!

"Do you sell many?" asked Pip, whilst the two girls ambled round the shop, pretending to look at everything.

"Only sold three this week," said the boy.

"All to cyclists?" asked Pip.

"How should I know?" said the boy. "The customers don't wheel their bikes into the shop with them!"

Pip didn't quite know what to say next. He joined the girls, and they all examined the contents of the rather interesting shop.

"You've got an awful lot of things here," said Daisy. "Do you remember all the prices and everything?"

" 'Course. I've got a good memory," said the boy. "At the end of the day I remember every blessed thing I've sold!"

"Gracious!" said Daisy admiringly. "I bet you don't remember every customer too!"

"Oh yes, I do," said the boy proudly. "Never forget a thing, I don't!"

"Well – I bet you don't remember the customers who bought the three hooters!" said Daisy, quick as a flash. Pip and Bets thought how clever she was!

" 'Couse I do," said the boy. "One was the fellow that lives down the road at Kosy-Kot. The second one was a fellow with rather queer eyes – one blue and one brown – I don't know his name and never saw him before. But I'd know him again all right. And the third one was a fat boy who seemed in a bit of a hurry."

"That was Fatty," thought the three children. Daisy smiled at the shop-boy. "What a memory you've got!" she said. "You really are a marvel. Well, we must be going. Got your hooter, Bets? Well, come on, then!"

They hurried out of the shop, rejoicing. The man at Kosy-Kot – and a man with odd eyes. They might be Clues, they really might!

Looking For More Clues

Pip was having a boring time in the sweet-shop. There was nothing to see outside, except the old man on the bench. Nobody went near him at all. Mr. Goon breathed heavily behind Pip, evidently finding the shop a very hot place to be in on this blazing day. Pip made his lemonade last out a long time and then, to Mr. Goon's annoyance, asked for an ice.

"You children seem to live here," said Mr. Goon, at last.

"You seem to, as well," said Pip. "Nice shop, isn't it?"

Mr. Goon didn't think so at all. He was sick and tired of the shop – but it was the best place to watch that old man from, no doubt about that!

"You look hot," said Pip sympathetically. "Why don't you go for a row on the river, Mr. Goon? It would be cool there. Seems a pity to spend all your holiday cooped up here."

Mr. Goon gave one of his snorts. He wasn't on holiday. He was on a case, a most important case. And for reasons of his own he had to wear plain clothes. But he couldn't explain all that to this irritating boy. Mr. Goon wished Pip was a mosquito. Then he would slap at him, and finish him off.

Bets came in next, and Pip was very glad to see her. "Going to have an ice?" he said. "Well, sorry I can't wait with you, Bets. So long!"

He went out and, to Mr. Goon's annoyance, yet another of those children, Bets this time, settled down at the window-table, obviously intending to be there for some time. Bets was afraid of the policeman, so she kept her back to him and said nothing at all, but kept a sharp eye on the old man opposite on the bench. She thought how bored poor Fatty must be!

Fatty had a coughing fit, and Bets watched in alarm. The cough seemed so very real that she felt sure poor Fatty must be getting a terrible cold.

Then Fatty had a fit of the sniffles, and hunted all over himself for a handkerchief, at last producing a violent red one. Then he got up and hobbled round a bit, as if he had got stiff with sitting. Nobody in the world would have guessed he was anything but a poor, stiff old man.

Bets enjoyed the performance immensely. She knew that Fatty was putting it on for her benefit. Fatty liked little Bets' admiration, and he was pondering whether or not he should actually light the pipe he had filled, and try smoking it. That would send Bets into fits!

But he didn't dare to. He had tried already and it had made him feel very sick. So he contented himself with putting the filled pipe in his mouth unlighted, and keeping it there.

All the Find-Outers were glad when that day was over. It really began to be very boring, taking turns at sitting in the sweet-shop, and watching for something that didn't happen. As for Fatty, he was terribly bored.

"Tomorrow I'm going to supply myself with plenty of newspapers to read," he said. "I simply can't spend hours filling pipes and coughing and sniffing. And all for nothing too. Not a soul passed me a message or anything."

"We found out something interesting at the hooter-shop, though," said Bets, and she told Fatty about the two men who had bought hooters that week.

"One who lives at Kosy-Kot, and one man with odd eyes," she said. "The boy didn't know where he lived. And the third person who bought a hooter was you, of course."

"Has that shop only sold three hooters all these months, then?" said Fatty, surprised.

"Well, they've only just got them in," said Pip." "That's why. So, if that fellow who spoke to you the other day on the bench *is* a member of the gang, he's either living at Kosy-Kot – or he's wandering about somewhere with odd eyes – one blue and one brown!"

79

"We'd better try Kosy-Kot first," said Fatty, pleased. "You did well, Find-Outers. How did you get all this information?"

"Well, Daisy did, really," said Pip and he told Fatty how it had happened. Fatty banged Daisy on the back.

"Jolly good," he said. "Very quick-witted. Now – who's going to tackle Kosy-Kot?"

"Isn't it a frightful name?" said Pip. "Why do people choose names like that? Can't we go down into the village and find it tomorrow morning? It's too late now."

"Right," said Fatty. "We will. I shan't have to masquerade as that old fellow till the afternoon, so I can come with you. Meet at Pip's tomorrow morning, ten o'clock sharp."

So, at ten o'clock, they were all there, Buster too. They set off to find Kosy-Kot. They met a postman and he told them where it was.

They soon found it. It was a little bungalow set in a trim little garden. At the back was a shed.

"I bet that's where they keep the bicycles," said Fatty. "Now – how can we get a peep inside?"

"I know!" said Pip. "I've got a ball. I could chuck it into the garden, and then we could go and ask if we might get it back – and you could peep into the shed, Fatty. If a bike is there with a hooter on, we'll wait about for the man who lives here, and see if we recognize him as the one who spoke to you, and had a bike with a hooter. We might recognize the bike too, if we see it."

This seemed a good and simple plan. So Pip proceeded to carry it out. He threw the ball wildly, and it

80

flew into the garden of Kosy-Kot, actually hitting against the bicycle-shed.

"Blow!" said Pip loudly. "My ball's gone into that garden."

"We'll go and ask if we may get it," said Daisy. So into the gate they went and up to the front door.

A woman opened it. "Please, our ball has gone into your garden," said Pip. "May we get it?"

"Yes, but don't tread on any of the beds," said the woman, and shut the door. The children went round to the back of the house. To their annoyance they saw a man there, digging. He stared at them.

"What do you kids want?"

"Oh – excuse us, please, but your wife said we might come and get our ball," said Fatty, politely. "I hope you don't mind."

"Well, get it, then," said the man, and went on digging. Fatty made for the shed and pretended to hunt round about. The door was open and he looked inside. It was full of garden tools and old sacks – but there was no bike there at all. How annoying!

"Haven't you found it?" said the man, and came over to look too. Then Fatty gave an exclamation and picked up the ball. He looked at the neat little shed.

"Useful sheds those, aren't they?" he said. "Jolly good for bikes. Wish I had one like that."

"Oh, I don't use it for bikes," said the man. "We haven't any. I use it for my garden tools."

"Oh," said Fatty. "Well – thank you for letting us get our ball. We'll be going now."

They went out into the road and crossed over to talk. "Hasn't got a bike! But that boy at the shop distinctly said that the man at Kosy-Kot bought a hooter," said

Bets indignantly. "He *must* have got a bike. Why should he pretend he hasn't got one?"

"It's a bit suspicious," said Pip. They walked on, puzzled. Suddenly, round the corner, they heard the noise of a hooter! Parp-parp! Parp-parp! The children clutched at one another, thrilled. A hooter! Perhaps it belonged to the man with odd eyes! Perhaps it would be his bicycle coming round the corner!

But, round the corner, ridden at a tremendous pace, came a child on a tricycle. He ran right into Fatty, who gave a yell, and hopped round on one leg, holding his right foot in his hand.

"You little idiot! What did you come round the corner like that for?" yelled Fatty.

"Well, I hooted!" said the little boy indignantly. "Didn't you hear me? I hooted like this."

And he pressed the rubber hooter on his tricycle and it parp-parped loudly. "It's a new hooter," he said. "My Daddy bought it for me. You should have got out of the way when you heard me coming round the corner."

"We weren't expecting a tricycle," said Pip. "We thought the hooter was on a bike, coming along the road, not on the pavement."

"Well, I'm sorry," said the little boy, beginning to pedal again. "But I did hoot. I hoot at every corner. Like this."

Parp-parp went the hooter and the five children watched the little boy pedal swiftly down the pavement then cross the road, and disappear into the gate of Kosy-Kot.

"I feel like saying 'Gah!'" said poor Fatty. "Wasting our time looking for a hooter that's on a child's tricycle – and getting my foot run over!"

"Never mind," said Bets consolingly. "You'll be able *really* to limp this afternoon, when you're the old man again."

They all went back to Pip's. It didn't seem any use trying to find the owner of the other hooter. They couldn't possibly go round looking at every one in Peterswood to see who had odd eyes. It was very disappointing about the tricycle.

"I think this is a very *slow* sort of mystery," said Bets. "It will be time to go back to school again before we've even *begun* to solve it!"

"What's the date?" said Pip. "Let me see – it must be the seventh of September – no, the eighth. Gracious, we really haven't much more time!"

"Perhaps something will happen soon," said Larry hopefully. "You know how sometimes things sort of boil up and get terribly exciting all of a sudden."

"Well, it's time this one did," said Fatty. "It's been in the refrigerator long enough!"

Every one laughed. "I wouldn't mind sitting in a frig myself," said Daisy. "Let's get our bathing things and go and bathe in the river. I'm so awfully hot."

So down to the river they went, and were soon splashing about happily. Fatty, of course, was a very fine swimmer, and could swim right across the river and back. Bets splashed happily in the shallow water. The others swam about lazily just out of their depth.

Bets thought she would swim out to them. So off she went, striking out valiantly. She didn't see a punt coming smoothly through the water, and before she could save herself, she felt a sharp blow on her shoulder, and screamed.

The punt slid on, unable to stop, but a boat follow-

"You're all right, aren't you?"

ing behind, swung round, and a man caught hold of her and held her.

"You're all right, aren't you?" he said, bending over her. "Can you swim?"

"Yes," gasped Bets, striking out again. "Fatty! Fatty! Come here quickly!"

The others swam over to the frightened little girl. They helped her to the shore and she gazed after the distant boat, and gulped.

"Oh," she said, "oh, I've missed the most wonderful Clue! But I couldn't help it! Oh, Fatty, the man in that boat had odd eyes – one blue and one brown. I couldn't help noticing them when he caught hold of my shoulder. And now the boat is gone – and I never even noticed its name!"

"Oh, *Bets*!" said every one, and Bets looked ready to cry. "Didn't you notice what colour it was, or anything?" asked Larry.

Bets shook her head. "No – I suppose I was too frightened. Oh, I'm so sorry. It was such a wonderful Clue – and a Suspect, too – and I've lost them both!"

Something Happens At Last

That afternoon things really began to happen. Fatty disguised himself once more as the old man (who was keeping remarkably out of the way), and went to the bench in the village street as usual. He limped most realistically this time, because his foot had swollen up from being run over by the tricycle.

He had provided himself with plenty of newspapers

to read, and he sat down as carefully as ever, letting out a little groan as he did so.

In the sweet-shop opposite sat Mr. Goon, clad as usual in flannel trousers and a cream shirt open at the neck. He looked extremely hot, and was beginning to long for some bad weather – frost and snow if possible! Mr. Goon had never felt so hot in his life as in this blazing summer.

Larry went into the shop and sat down to order lemonade. Mr. Goon was getting used to the fact that one or other of the Find-Outers always seemed to be there. He took no notice of Larry. He just propped his paper up in front of him, and kept a watchful eye on the old fellow nodding on the bench across the street.

It looked as if Fatty had gone sound asleep. Larry yawned and wished he could go to sleep too. Then he noticed something. A man was standing in the shady doorway of a near-by shop, and he seemed to be watching the old man. Was he thinking of giving him a message?

Mr. Goon also spotted the man, and sat up straight. The man looked up and down the street, and lighted a cigarette, puffing hard at it.

The village was empty and deserted on this hot afternoon. A car drove by and disappeared. A dog ambled round a corner, lay down, and fell asleep. Larry and Mr. Goon watched the silent man breathlessly.

The man sauntered across the road and stood for a few minutes looking in the window of a wireless shop. Then he strolled over to the bench and sat down near the old man.

Fatty was pretending to be asleep, but he spotted the man out of the corner of his eye, and something told him that the man was no chance companion. He was there for a purpose. Fatty jerked himself upright as if he had suddenly awakened, and sniffled loudly. He wiped his nose with his sleeve and then leaned over his stick again. Then he coughed his dreadful cough.

"Awful cough you've got!" said the man. Fatty took no notice, remembering that he was deaf. He coughed again.

"AWFUL COUGH YOU'VE GOT!" repeated the man. Fatty turned, put his hand behind his ear and croaked out a familiar word, "Wassat?"

The stranger laughed. He took out his cigarette case and offered the old man a cigarette. There was only one left in the case. As soon as Fatty had taken it, the man filled his case from a packet.

"Thank you, sir," croaked Fatty, and put the cigarette into his pocket. His heart beat fast. He felt sure that there must be some kind of message in the cigarette. What would it be? He did not dare to look closely at that man, but hoped that Larry was taking note of all his clothes and everything.

Larry was. And so was Mr. Goon! Both were mentally repeating the same things. "Grey flannel suit. Blue shirt. Black shoes. No tie. Grey felt hat. Moustache. Tall. Slim. Long nose. Small eyes."

The man got up to go. He disappeared quite quickly round the corner. Fatty thought that he, too, had better disappear quickly, before Mr. Goon could get hold of him and get the cigarette-message, whatever it was, away from him. So he, too, got up, and with most surprising agility in such an old man, he shot round another corner.

And then he saw something most aggravating! Coming towards him was the *real* old man, corduroy trousers, dirty muffler and all! He was out for a walk, though he did not mean to go and sit on the bench.

Fatty could not risk being seen by the old man, for he guessed he would be amazed and alarmed at the sight of his double. So he popped into the nearest gate and hid himself under a bush.

He was only just in time! Mr. Goon came round the corner with a rush – and almost bumped into the real old man! He clutched him tightly.

"Ha! Got you! Now you give me that cigarette right away!"

The old man looked most alarmed. He shrank away from the red-faced Mr. Goon, not in the least knowing who he was, for he did not recognize the policeman dressed in plain clothes.

"Where's that cigarette?" panted Mr. Goon.

"Wassat?" croaked the old man. Goon heard footsteps behind him and saw Larry. Larry was horrified to see what he thought was Fatty in the clutches of the policeman. He stayed nearby to see what was going to happen. The old man tried feebly to get away from Goon, but the policeman held on grimly.

"You let go," said the old fellow. "I'll get the police, see? Catching hold of me like this! I'll get the police!"

"It's the police that have got *you*," said Goon, shaking him. "I'm GOON! GOON the POLICEMAN! And I want that CIGARETTE!"

This was too much for the poor old man. He almost fell down in fright. He hadn't the faintest idea what Goon wanted him for, nor did he know why Goon kept on shouting for a cigarette.

"Have my pipe," said the old fellow, trying to get it

out of his pocket. "Have my pipe and let me go. I ain't done nothing."

Mr. Goon snorted, caught hold of the old fellow by the collar of his coat and marched him down the street. "You can come to the police-station with me," he said. "And I'll search you there and get that cigarette! See!"

Larry watched them go, feeling rather scared, for he still thought it was Fatty that Mr. Goon had got. He had the fright of his life when he suddenly saw another old man peering out from under a bush at him!

"Larry! Have they gone?" said this old man, in Fatty's voice. Larry almost jumped out of his skin.

"*Fatty!* I thought it was *you* that Goon was taking away! Golly, I'm glad it wasn't."

Fatty came out from under the bush. "The real old man happened to come walking up here just as I was hurrying to get away from Goon!" said Fatty, with a grin. "So I hopped in at this gate and hid, and Goon grabbed the old fellow and ordered him to give up the cigarette he hadn't got. Phew! That was a jolly narrow shave!"

"Fatty! Is there a message in that cigarette?" said Larry eagerly. "Can we find out? I saw that fellow give you one. I watched him for a long time. So did Goon."

"Let's go to Pip's," said Fatty. "We're safer there than anywhere, because his garden is so big. Don't walk with me. Go in front, and when you come to a corner, whistle if you want to warn me."

Larry walked on in front. He did not whistle at any corners, because there seemed to be nobody about in Peterswood at all that hot September afternoon. In ten minutes Fatty was safely in Pip's summer-house. He did not strip off his old clothes, because he had no others to change into. He waited there whilst Larry went off to collect the others, and he hoped that no grown-ups would think of poking their noses into the summer-house that afternoon. They would not be pleased to find a dirty old tramp there!

Fatty longed to examine the cigarette and see what was inside it. But he waited patiently till the others came tearing up the path, pouring into the little summer-house with excited faces.

"Fatty! Larry's told us all about it! What's the message? Is there one in the cigarette? Have you looked?"

"Of course not. I waited for you all," said Fatty. He took the cigarette from his pocket. It was rather a stout, fat one. It had tobacco at each end – but when Fatty had scraped out as much tobacco as he could, he found that the middle of the cigarette was not made of tobacco at all – but was stuffed with a tight roll of paper!

"Oh!" said Bets, almost too excited to breathe. "A secret message! Oh, Fatty!"

Fatty unrolled the paper. He flattened it with his hand. The five of them leaned over it, their breaths hot against one another's cheeks. Buster tried in vain to see what all the excitement was about, but for once in a way nobody took the slightest notice of him!

The message proved to be very puzzling and disappointing. All it said was:

"One tin black boot-polish.
One pound rice.
One pound tea.
Two pounds syrup.
One bag flour."

90

"Why! It's only a grocery list!" said Daisy. "Just like Mother often gives me and Larry when we go shopping for her. Whatever does it mean, Fatty?"

"I don't know," said Fatty. "It must mean something. I hope it's not in a secret code."

"What's a secret code?" asked Bets.

"Oh, a way of writing messages so that only the persons receiving them know what they mean," said Fatty. "But somehow I don't think this is a code. After all, that old man had got to read it and understand it, and I'm quite sure he hasn't brains enough to understand a code."

"Then could there be another message, but written in secret ink?" said Pip suddenly. "You know how you taught us to write secret messages, in between the lines of an ordinary letter, don't you, Fatty? Well, could there be a message written between these lines, in secret ink?"

"Yes, there could," said Fatty. "And that's what I think we shall find! Good for you, Pip. Can you go and get a warm iron? If we run it over the paper, the secret message will show up."

Pip ran off. Gladys was actually ironing in the kitchen, and though she was very surprised to think that Pip should want to borrow the warm iron to take into the garden for a minute, she let him. He came tearing up to the summer-house with it in his hand.

"I've got it!" he said. "Here you are. Put the paper out flat on the wooden table. That's right. Now I'll run the iron over it."

He ran the warm iron over the spread-out bit of paper. Then he lifted it off and looked at the message. "There's another one coming up, look – between the lines of the other!" squealed Daisy, in excitement. "Iron it again, Pip, quick! Oh, this is too thrilling for words!"

Pip ironed the paper again – and this time another message showed up very clearly indeed. The words came up, looking a queer grey-brown colour, and began to fade almost as soon as the children had made them out.

> "Tell Number 3. Waxworks, Tuesday,
> nine p.m. – Number 5."

"Golly!" said Pip. "Look at that! Tell Number 3 – that must be one of the gang. And Number 5 must be another."

"Waxworks, Tuesday, nine p.m." said Fatty, and his eyes gleamed. "So that's one of their meeting-places. Down in the Waxworks Hall, where all those figures are. *Now* we know something!"

"We really do," said Bets. "What are they meeting about, Fatty?"

"I don't know – but I shall find out," said Fatty. "Because – I shall be there on Tuesday night!"

In Mr. Goon's Clutches

The children were full of excitement when they heard Fatty say this. "What! Go down to the Waxworks, and attend the gang meeting!" said Larry. "You wouldn't dare! You'd be discovered, however well you hid yourself!"

"It's the only way of finding out who all the gang are," said Fatty. "I shall see them, hear them talk and plan – my word, this *is* a bit of luck!"

"No wonder Goon wanted to get hold of that cigarette from the old man," said Daisy. "He would give anything to have this message!"

"He'll wonder what the old chap's done with it!" said Fatty, with a grin. "He'll have searched him from top to toe – but he won't have found that cigarette!"

They talked excitedly for some time and then Fatty said he really must go home and get out of his hot, smelly old-man clothes. The others walked down to the gate with him, leaving an angry Buster tied up in the summer-house.

Meanwhile Mr. Goon had had a most disappointing time. He had found no cigarette at all on the old man. He was angry and puzzled, and he shouted at the old fellow, getting redder and redder in the face.

"You can stay here till you tell me what you did with that cigarette, see?" he yelled. "I'll lock you up till you do. Now then – are you going to tell me?"

The old chap had turned sulky. He knew nothing of any cigarette, he hadn't been sitting on the bench, he didn't know what the bad-tempered policeman was talking about. So he sulked and said nothing at all, which made Goon madder than ever.

"Right!" said Goon at last, getting up. "I'll talk to you some more tomorrow."

He went home and changed into his uniform. Then he decided to go and see "that boy Larry" and ask him if he, too, had noticed the man giving the old fellow a cigarette that afternoon. Mr. Goon couldn't help being puzzled by the old chap's firm denials of any knowledge of a cigarette. But Larry must have seen the gift, and would bear witness to it.

But Larry was out. "Try at the Hilton's," said Larry's mother. "Oh, I do hope the children haven't been misbehaving themselves, Mr. Goon."

"Er no – for a wonder, no, Mam," said Mr. Goon, and went off majestically.

He arrived at Pip's just as the children were escorting Fatty, still disguised as the old man, out of the front gate. Fatty stared at Goon, and Goon stared back disbelievingly. What! Hadn't he just locked that old man up? And here he was again, free, and walking about! Mr. Goon began to feel as if he was in a peculiarly unpleasant dream.

"Er – good evening, Mr. Goon," said Larry. Mr. Goon took no notice of him.

"Here, you!" he said, grabbing at Fatty's arm. "How did you get out? Haven't I just locked you up? What are things a-coming to, I'd like to know! Here I've just locked you up and I meet you walking into me, bold as brass!"

Mr. Goon looked so amazed and disbelieving that Fatty badly wanted to laugh. He was at a loss to know what to say.

"Wassat?" he said at last, putting his hand behind his ear.

That was too much for Mr. Goon. He caught hold of Fatty's collar and marched him quickly up the lane.

"You've been 'wassating' me long enough!" said the annoyed Mr. Goon. "I don't know how you got out – but I do know you're going in again – and this time I'll lock the door on you meself! And there you'll stay till you see sense if it takes you a month!"

Fatty didn't like this at all. He debated whether or not to let Mr. Goon into the secret of his disguise. But

94

before he had made up his mind, he was at the police-station. Mr. Goon was unlocking a door, and Fatty was being pushed into the dark, narrow little room behind.

And in it was the real old man! He stared at Fatty and Fatty stared at him. The old chap let out a howl. He was beginning to feel he must be mad. Why, here was himself staring at him! What was happening?

Mr. Goon heard the howl and looked into the room – and then he saw the *two* old men! Exactly alike. As like as peas in a pod. Mr. Goon sat down heavily on a chair and mopped his forehead with a big handkerchief. He felt dazed. What with vanishing cigarettes, men that got locked up and then got out – and now two old men exactly alike – well, Mr. Goon began to feel that he must be lying asleep and dreaming in his own bed at home, and he fervently hoped that he would soon wake up.

"Lemme get out of here!" said the real old man, and tried to push past Mr. Goon. But the policeman caught hold of him. He wasn't going to have any more disappearings. He was Going to Get to the Bottom of Things.

Fatty saw that things had gone far enough, and he did not like the thought of his parents knowing that he was locked up at the police-station. So he spoke to Mr. Goon in his ordinary voice, and gave the poor man another terrible shock.

"Mr. Goon! I'm not really an old man. I'm Frederick Trotteville."

Mr. Goon's mouth fell open. He gulped once or twice, staring at Fatty as if he couldn't believe his eyes. Fatty twitched off his beard, and then Mr. Goon did indeed see that it was Fatty. He dragged him out of the

95

dark little room, slammed and locked the door, and took Fatty into an office.

"Now you just tell me the meaning of all this here!" he said.

"Well," said Fatty, "it's a long story, but I'll tell you everything, Mr. Goon," and he launched into the tale of all that the Find-Outers had done, and how he had disguised himself as the old man, and sat there to trap a message from the gang.

"What about that cigarette?" said Mr. Goon when he had got his breath back a bit. "What about that? That's a most important thing!"

"Is it really?" said Fatty, in pretended surprise. "Well, we undid the cigarette, of course, Mr. Goon, and inside we found nothing of importance at all, really – just a silly grocery list. We were terribly disappointed."

Fatty did not mean to tell Mr. Goon what he and the others had discovered in the message – the few lines in secret ink. No, he would keep that to himself, and go to the meeting on Tuesday night, and see what he could find out. *He* wanted to solve the Mystery, he, Fatty, the chief of the Find-Outers. He did not stop to think whether it was dangerous or not.

Mr. Goon grabbed hold of the message. He spread it out. He frowned. He read it through two or three times. "Must be a code," he said. "I'll look up my codebook. You leave this to me."

"Er – well – I'll be going now," said Fatty, after watching Mr. Goon frowning at the list of groceries for a few minutes.

"If you hadn't given me this here bit of paper, I'd have locked you up," said Mr. Goon. "Interfering with the Law. That's what you're always doing, you five kids. Ho, yes, I know you think you've got a fine friend in Inspector Jenks, but one of these days you'll find he's fed up with you, see? And I'll get my promotion and be a Big Noise, and then just you look out!"

"Oh, I *will* look out," said Fatty earnestly. "Thanks for warning me, Mr. Goon. Er – what about that old fellow? Are you still going to keep him locked up?"

"Yes, I am," said Mr. Goon. "And your own common sense will tell you why – that's always supposing you've got any, which I very much doubt – I don't want him warning the gang that I'm on their track. If he's here, under my nose, he can't do much warning."

"I think you're quite right, Mr. Goon," said Fatty solemnly. "I couldn't agree with you more. I think –"

"I'm tired of you," said Mr. Goon. "You clear-orf double-quick, before I change my mind about locking you up. I'm Right Down Tired of you. Messing about – interfering – dressing up – Gah!"

Fatty scuttled off. He went home and quickly changed out of his old-man clothes, and then shot up to Pip's to tell every one what had happened.

"I had to give him the cigarette message, worse luck," he said. "It was the only thing to keep him quiet. But I don't believe he'll make head or tail of it, and I bet he won't test it for a secret message as we did. You should have seen his face when he pushed me into the same room as the real old man, and saw two of us there! I thought he would go up in smoke!"

The others roared. They were most relieved to see Fatty back safe and sound. Bets had been imagining him locked up in a dreary cell, with only bread and water.

"He's keeping the old man under his eye for a few

days," said Fatty, "in case he gets the wind up about all this, and warns the other members of the gang. I'm pleased he's doing that. I expect the Meeting will wonder why Number 3 doesn't turn up on Tuesday, whoever he is. Well, they'll have to wonder!"

"I think it's awfully dangerous for you to go down to the Waxworks on Tuesday," said Daisy. "I do, really. I think you ought to go and tell the Inspector about it, Fatty."

"Oh no," said Fatty. "I want us to solve this Mystery before we see the Inspector again. I shall be quite safe."

"I don't see how you can say that," said Larry, who agreed with Daisy that it might be dangerous. "The men will surely not be fools enough to hold their Meeting without being certain there's no spy there."

"They won't discover *me*," said Fatty. "I shall wear a disguise!"

"I don't see how that will help you," said Larry. "Even if you are in disguise, you'll be a stranger to the men, and they'll want to know who you are."

"I shan't be a stranger to them," said Fatty, exasperatingly. "Nor to you, either."

The others stared at him. "What do you mean?" said Pip at last. "What are you getting at?"

"I shall be somebody the gang have seen often enough before, if they have held their other meetings in the Waxworks Hall. They'll know me so well they won't even look at me!"

"What do you *mean*?" said Daisy, getting annoyed. "Don't talk in these silly riddles."

"Well," said Fatty, and he lowered his voice to a mysterious whisper, "well – I shall be disguised as one of the waxworks, silly! Napoleon, I think, because I'm pretty plump, and so was he!"

There was a complete silence. All the Find-Outers stared at Fatty in the greatest admiration. What an idea! No member of the gang would suspect any of the wax-work figures! Bets could just imagine Fatty standing stiff and straight as the waxwork Napoleon, staring fixedly in front of him – seeing and hearing everything.

"What a really marvellous idea!" said Larry, at last. "Oh, Fatty – I should never have thought of that if I'd thought for a month. You'll be right in the lions' den – and they won't even *smell* you!"

"It *is* rather a good idea, isn't it?" said Fatty, swelling up a little. "That's one thing about me, you know – I've always got plenty of ideas. My form-master said only last term that my imagination was . . ."

But the others didn't in the least want to hear what Fatty's form-master had said. They wanted to talk about Tuesday night and what Fatty was going to do.

Tuesday night! Bets thrilled every time she thought of it. This Mystery was really getting too exciting for words. Oooh – Tuesday night!

A Very Bold Idea

That week-end dragged along very slowly indeed. Tuesday was such a long time in coming! The only thing that enlivened it at all was that on the two or three occasions when the children met Mr. Goon, Fatty had his hooter tucked under his coat, and sounded it as soon as they passed the policeman.

This made him jump, and he looked round in hope

of seeing the cyclist who had once stopped and spoken to the old man. But he never did, of course. He hailed the children suspiciously the third time it happened.

"Did you hear that hooter?" he asked. They all nodded vigorously.

"Did you see a bike going by then?" said the policeman.

"A bike? All by itself with a hooter?" asked Pip, and the others grinned.

"Gah!" said Mr. Goon, enranged as usual. "You clearorf! I wouldn't put it past you to carry one of them hooters about, just to annoy me, like!"

"He's getting quite bright, isn't he?" said Larry, as they walked off. "I shouldn't be surprised if he does get promotion one of these days. He's really trying to use those brains of his a bit. We'd better not hoot any more when we pass him. He's quite likely to go and complain about us if we do – and ever since he went up to my house and asked for me the other day, Mother's been warning me not to get into trouble."

Fatty was preparing himself very earnestly for Tuesday night. He knew how important it was, and he also knew that, unless all his details were absolutely perfect, he might be in considerable danger.

He and the others spent a long time in the Waxworks, much to the surprise of the red-headed boy, for it was very hot in there, and not many people visited the little hall these blazing days.

But Fatty had to study the figure of Napoleon very carefully indeed. He meant to get into the hall somehow on Tuesday evening, and dress himself up in Napoleon's clothes. Would they fit him? He asked Daisy what she thought.

"Yes, I should think they'd fit you very well," she said, considering first Napoleon and then Fatty. "You had better take a few safety-pins in case something doesn't quite meet. The hat will be fine – just your size, I should think. What about hair, Fatty?"

"I can manage that all right," said Fatty. "I rather think my own will do, if I smarm it down a bit, and pull a few pieces out in front, like old Napoleon has got. An er – I don't know what you think – but – er – I'm not really *unlike* Napoleon in features, am I?"

The others stared at him. "Well," said Pip honestly, "I can't see any likeness at *all*. Not the slightest."

"Except that you're both fat," said Daisy.

"Do you *want* to look like Napoleon?" said Bets in surprise. "I don't think he looks very nice, really. And I don't like those men that go about thinking they want to conquer the whole world. Napoleon must have been very brainy, of course, and *you're* brainy, Fatty. But, except that you're fat and brainy, I don't see that you're very like Napoleon."

Fatty gave it up. He stared once more at the figure of Napoleon, in its grand uniform, cocked hat, medals, epaulettes, and stars. It was a fine uniform and Fatty was longing to get into it. Well, he hadn't got long to wait now.

He tried to memorize exactly at what angle Napoleon wore his hat, exactly how he held his hands, exactly how he stared so blankly in front of him. Napoleon fortunately stood in the very front row of figures, so Fatty, as Napoleon, would be able to hear and see everything very well indeed. A little shiver went down his back when he thought of standing there, perfectly still,

Fatty examined Napoleon very carefully

listening to the plans of the gang, and memorizing their appearance.

It was a very bold idea indeed. Not one of the other Find-Outers would have dared to do it. But Fatty, of course, would dare anything. Bets thought that he wouldn't even turn a hair if he met a roaring lion, the kind she met in her bad dreams, and which scared her terribly. Fatty would probably speak to it kindly and pat it, and the lion would lie down and roll over for Fatty to tickle it on its tummy – like Buster did!

The red-headed boy, curious at their sudden intense interest in Napoleon, came over and joined them.

"What's exciting about *him*?" he said. "Who is he? Oh – Napoleon. What was he? Some sort of soldier?"

"Don't you *know*?" said Bets, in astonishment. "Didn't you learn history at school?"

"I've never been to school," said the red-headed boy. "I belong to the Fair, and us kids hardly ever go to school unless we have to. We move about from place to place, you see, and before we're popped into some school, we've moved on again. I can read, but I can't write."

"Why are you in the Waxwork Show?" asked Fatty. "Does this hall belong to the Fair people?"

"Oh no – they've only hired it," said the boy. "The Waxworks belong to my uncle. He's the fellow that runs the Hoopla. I used to help him with that, but now I have to do the Waxworks, and it's jolly dull."

Fatty wondered if any of the Fair people were in the gang of thieves. It seemed very likely. Well, he would know on Tuesday night.

The children went and studied other figures carefully too, so that the red-headed boy wouldn't get suspicious about their sudden interest in Napoleon. They had a good look at the wax figure of the policeman as well. He really did look a bit like Mr. Goon! There he stood, on the second step, not far from Napoleon, his helmet on perfectly straight, the strap round the chin, and the belt a little tight.

The red-headed boy disappeared out-of-doors for a minute. Fatty at once went back to Napoleon and studied the clothes well, to make sure that he could take them off the wax figure fairly easily.

"Hope they're not *stuck* on in any way," he said to the others anxiously. Daisy pulled at them.

"Oh no," she said. "They are put on just like ours – and look, the trousers are held by braces. You'll be all right, Fatty. But you'll have to be here long before nine, or you'll never have time to undress yourself *and* Napoleon and then dress yourself up again."

"I wish you wouldn't, really, Fatty," said Bets, looking up at him with scared eyes. "I shall hate to think of you standing so near the gang – whatever would they do to you if they discovered you?"

"They won't," said Fatty. "I shan't give myself away, you may be sure of that. I've already been practising standing still for ages, in my bedroom, in exactly that position. Buster simply can't understand it. He does all he can to make me move!"

The others laughed. They could quite well picture Fatty standing solemnly in his room, perfectly still, with a most astonished Buster trying in vain to get a movement or a sound out of him!

"Come on – let's go now," said Fatty. "It's most frightfully hot in here. Hallo – there's Goon – and in uniform again! He looks better in uniform than in plain clothes, I must say. Not that he's much to look at in either!"

Mr. Goon was standing just outside the Waxworks Hall, apparently about to go in. He scowled when he saw the children. Funny how those kids always seemed to turn up everywhere!

"What are you doing here?" he asked, in a suspicious voice.

"Passing the time away, Mr. Goon, just passing the time," said Fatty airily. "What are *you* doing here? Is your holiday over? You must miss your little trips to the sweet-shop."

Buster was on the lead, or he would certainly have darted at his enemy. But Fatty, seeing the black look on Mr. Goon's face, hastily dragged him away.

"Wonder what he's done with that grocery list!" said Daisy, with a giggle. "Put it with his Clues, I expect. Well, we know more about that than he does!"

Bets wanted to go down by the river, so the others went, too, meaning to walk home by the river-path. Bets stared hard at every one in boats, and Pip noticed her.

"Why ever are you glaring at every one who's in a boat?" he asked.

"I'm not glaring," said Bets. "I'm just looking to see if I can spot anyone with odd eyes, that's all. I did see the odd-eyed man in a boat, you know, when that punt knocked against me – and I might quite well see him again."

"What would you do if you did?" demanded Pip. "Jump in and arrest him?"

"It's quite a good idea of Bets," said Fatty, always quick to defend the little girl. "After all, if the man was

105

in a boat once, he might be again. And if we saw him on the river we could get the name of the boat, and, if it was privately owned, we could find out the name of the owner."

"The only thing is – people go by so quickly that it's difficult to see if their eyes are odd or not," said Bets.

"I say, Fatty, how are you going to get your face all pink like Napoleon's?" asked Larry looking at Fatty's very brown face.

"Easy," said Fatty. "I shall put a little layer of pink wax all over my face and let it set. I know how to do it. It's in a book I've got."

Fatty had the most extraordinary collection of books. He seemed to be able to find out from them anything he wanted.

"You'll have to do that before you set out, won't you?" said Daisy. Fatty nodded.

"Yes. Larry will have to go with me if the night isn't dark enough to hide me, and warn me if any one is coming who might be likely to spot me. But now that there's no moon, I ought not to be noticed much in the twilight."

"I do want Tuesday to come!" said Bets. "I really can hardly wait! I wish I was going to see you all dressed up as Napoleon, Fatty. You'll look simply grand. Oh, Tuesday, hurry up and come!"

Tuesday Night At Last

Tuesday night did come at last. For once in a way it was a cloudy night, and it almost looked as if the longed-for rain was coming. It was a little cooler, and every one was thankful.

"How are you going to manage about your father and mother tonight?" asked Pip. "I mean – you want to set off about 7.30, don't you? And that's the time you have dinner with them."

"They're away for a couple of nights," said Fatty. "Bit of luck, that. Larry, you come to dinner with me, and we'll have it at seven, together. Then you can walk down with me to the Hall, to make sure no one will see me."

"Right," said Larry. "I will. Wish I was going to come into the Hall with you, too, and see everything. Will you come back and tell us what's happened, Fatty, even if it's awfully late? I'll keep awake."

"All right. But I'd better not go to Pip's," said Fatty. "Mrs. Hilton is sure to hear me if I call up to Pip. Her room is just nearby."

"Oh, *Fatty*! We can't possibly wait till the morning!" cried Bets.

"You'll have to," said Fatty. "I can't go round to you all and tell you what's happened. Anyway, you'll be fast asleep, little Bets!"

"I shan't. I shan't sleep a wink all night," said Bets.

The day dragged by very slowly. At half-past six Fatty left Pip's, with Larry, and the two of them went to Fatty's house. They were to have dinner early, at seven – then their adventure would begin. All the children felt excited, but only Fatty did not show it. He appeared to be as calm as ever.

The two boys made a very good meal indeed. Then Fatty put the pink stuff on his face and after that they set out to go down to the river. They meant to take the path over the fields, then go by the water-side, and so come to the Fair without meeting a lot of people.

They arrived at the Waxworks Hall. "How are you going to get in?" whispered Larry, suddenly seeing that the place was shut and in darkness.

"Didn't you spot me undoing the catch of one of the windows when we were here this morning?" whispered Fatty. "I'm going to get in there. I say – what about you coming in too, in case I get into difficulties over dressing? You can easily hop out of the window afterwards."

"Yes, I will," said Larry, pleased at the idea of watching Fatty dress himself as Napoleon. "Where's the window?"

"It's this one," said Fatty, and looked cautiously round. "Anyone about? Not a soul! Here goes, then!"

He opened the window quietly, hauled himself up and dropped down into the hall. Larry followed. The boys shut the window carefully, in case any one noticed that it was open.

The hall wasn't dark, because a lamp from the Fair nearby shone into it, and gave a fint and rather eerie light to the still waxworks.

The boys looked round them. The figures somehow seemed more alive than in the daytime, and Larry gave a little shiver. Silly fancies crept into his head. Suppose wax figures came alive at night and walked and talked!

What a dreadful shock it would give him and Fatty!

"They all seem to be looking at us," whispered Larry. "They make me feel quite creepy. Look at Nelson – he's watching us all the time!"

"Idiot!" said Fatty, walking over to Napoleon. "Come on – help me to undress him, Larry."

It was a queer business, undressing the rather plump figure of the wax Napoleon. It wasn't easy, either, because Naopleon didn't help in any way! In fact, it almost seemed as if he quite deliberately tried to make things difficult for the two boys!

"If only he'd raise his arms a bit, or give a wriggle, or something," whispered Larry. "We could get his things off easily then. But he just makes himself as stiff as possible!"

Fatty chuckled. "I'd get a shock if he *did* raise his arms or wriggle!" he said. "I'd just as soon he didn't. There – his coat's off, thank goodness – but I've torn his high collar a bit. Now for his trousers."

Soon poor Napoleon stood stiff and straight in nothing but some kind of shapeless under-garment. The boys lifted him up and carried him to a cupboard. They put him inside and shut the door. Then Fatty proceeded to undress himself very quickly. He stuffed his own clothes into the cupboard with Napoleon.

Then, with Larry's help he put on Napoleon's clothes. They fitted him quite well, and he only had to use one of Daisy's safety-pins. He pulled on the coat, and the medals made a little jingling noise.

"Fatty! You look marvellous in that uniform!" said Larry, in admiration. "You honestly do! Now the hat – golly, it fits you as if it was made for you!"

Fatty made Larry hold up a small mirror and looked

109

at his face in it. It was all covered with pink, and looked very like the faces of the wax figures around. Fatty pulled a strand of hair on to his forehead, just like the one the wax Napoleon had had. Then he put his hand under his coat, stood absolutely still and stiff, and stared straight in front of him.

Larry couldn't find enough words of praise. "Nobody, *nobody* could possibly guess you weren't a wax figure!" he said. "You're marvellous, Fatty! Honestly, you're more of a wax figure than Napoleon was before! I wish you could see yourself, I really do. Golly, it's wonderful!"

Fatty was pleased. He beamed modestly at Larry, but not too broadly in case the wax on his face cracked a bit.

"It's only your eyes that are different from the other wax figures," said Larry. "They've got a proper light in them – the others haven't. Yours shine."

"Well, I hope they won't shine too much!" said Fatty. "Now, you'd better go, Larry, old boy. It's about half-past eight, isn't it? The men might be here early."

"Right," said Larry – and then he suddenly stood stock-still in fright. It sounded as if some one was fumbling at the door of the hall!

"Go, quickly!" said Fatty, in a whisper, and Larry fled, threading his way carefully between the silent figures till he came to the window at the back of the hall. He opened it cautiously, climbed up and dropped out, shutting it again at once. He dived under a bush and sat there, hardly daring to breathe, mopping his forehead with his handkerchief.

He pictured the gang walking in silently, and he felt glad he was not Fatty, all alone there, hidden in the rows of waxwork figures. Golly, he'd only got out just in time!

Fatty was waiting in the greatest excitement for the hall door to open. Who would come in? The leader of the gang? All the men? Would he know any of them?

The fumbling at the door went on. Somebody seemed to be having difficulty with the key. But at last it turned and the door opened quietly. Somebody stepped in, and shut the door – and locked it! Why lock it? Fatty was puzzled. Weren't the others coming in too, then?

The silent-footed person moved down the hall, and the light from the Fair lamp outside shone down on him. Fatty got a most tremendous shock.

It was Mr. Goon!

"Goon!" thought Fatty, and he almost fell off his step. "Old Clear-Orf! *Goon!* But – is he one of the gang then? Goon here, with the thieves! What's it all mean?"

Mr. Goon proceeded to do a few very peculiar things. He walked behind Fatty until he came to one of the wax figures. Fatty did not know which one, for he dared not move or turn round to see what Goon was doing.

Mr. Goon then lifted up the figure, and, panting noisily, carried it to a big window, where a voluminous curtain hung. Then Fatty was able to see which figure Mr. Goon was carrying.

It was the wax policeman! Mr. Goon carefully placed him behind the curtain, and then creaked back to the place where the wax figure had stood.

And, in a flash, Fatty understood everything. He almost groaned in disappointment.

"Of course – Goon has read the secret message in that grocery list after all – he found out, as we did, that a meeting of the Gang will be held here tonight – and he got the same brain-wave too. He thought he'd come and be one of the wax figures, and listen in to everything! Golly – he's got more brains and pluck than I'd have thought he had!"

Poor Fatty! It was a great shock and disappointment to him to know that the policeman would hear everything, and be able to solve the Mystery after all. He would know the Gang – and their plans – and would be able to arrest the whole lot of them at once!

But surely he wouldn't dare to tackle the whole gang single-handed? No – that couldn't be his plan. Then what was it? Fatty stood and puzzled his brains, angry and miserable to think that Goon should have been clever enough to think of exactly the same idea as the Find-Outers.

"But it was much more difficult for *me*," thought Fatty. "I had to undress the figure of Napoleon and dress myself up again – Goon only had to go and stand in the place of the wax policeman. We always did think that the wax figure was like Goon! Blow! Everything's spoilt."

Fatty would have given anything to turn round and see what Goon looked like, standing stiffly there some way behind him. Goon was breathing very heavily, as he always did when he was excited. Fatty wondered if he would remember to breathe quietly when the Gang came in! Then Goon did a little cough, and cleared his throat.

"Of course, he thinks there's nobody here at all," thought Fatty. "So it doesn't matter what noises he makes. I want to cough, myself – but I daren't, because Goon would be very suspicious at once. What a shock it would give him, to hear one of the waxworks cough.

112

I wonder if he'd get scared and go flying out of the hall at once! No, I don't think he would!"

Mr. Goon shuffled his feet a little and sniffed. Then he got out his handkerchief and blew his nose.

Fatty immediately wanted to blow his too! It was most irritating wanting to sniff and cough and blow his nose when he dared not make a single movement. Spoiling everything! Enjoying himself sniffing and coughing. Waiting for his Big Moment – and thinking of Promotion!

There came the sound of voices outside. Then a key was put into the door, and it opened. "Ho!" thought Fatty, "Mr. Goon had a duplicate key, had he? He made his plans well. Locked the door after him, too, so that the men shouldn't get suspicious, as they would have if the door had been unlocked!"

Four men came in. Fatty strained his eyes to try and see what their faces were like. But one and all wore soft hats pulled well down over their foreheads. They did not light a lamp, nor did they even use torches. The faint light from the Fair lamp outside seemed to be enough for them.

They got chairs and sat down. They waited for a while, saying nothing. Fatty wondered why. Then he knew.

"Where's Number Three?" said one of the men impatiently. "He ought to be here. Didn't you warn him, Number Five?"

"Yes, I sent him a message," said another man. "In a cigarette I gave to old Johnny. He'll turn up soon."

They waited in silence again. One of the men pulled out a watch and looked at it.

113

"Can't wait any longer," he said. "The job's on to-night."

"Tonight?" said another man. "Where? All of us in it this time, or not?"

"All of us," said the first man. "Except Number Three, as he's not here. It's the Castleton pearls to-night."

"Whew!" said two of the men. "Big stuff!"

"Very big," said the first man. "Now see here – these are the plans. You, Number Two, have got to drive the car, and you . . ."

Fatty and Mr. Goon watched and listened intently. Mr. Goon remembered not to breathe loudly, and as for Fatty, he was so excited that he hardly breathed at all. They heard all the details of the new robbery to be pulled off that night. But try as he would Fatty could not see clearly the face of any of the men at all.

He began to think hard. The men would soon be gone. Once they were gone he would get to the telephone and tell the Inspector all he knew – and the robbery could be stopped. Then he remembered Mr. Goon. Blow! Goon would be in charge of this, not Fatty.

Poor Mr. Goon was not feeling very happy just at that moment. He wanted to sneeze. He could feel it coming quite distinctly. He swallowed violently and wriggled his nose about. No – that sneeze meant to come. Whooosh-ooo!

It wasn't a very big sneeze, because Mr. Goon had tried most valiantly to stop it, and it came out in quite a gentlemanly manner. But it was enough to startle all the men, and Fatty too, almost out of their skins!

The men sprang to their feet at once, and looked all round the hall. "What was that? There's somebody here! Somebody spying on us!"

Fatty was suddenly frightened. The men's eyes gleamed under their hats, and he could hear a savage tone in the voice of the man who spoke. The boy kept absolutely still. Silly, idiotic old Goon, to give the game away like that!

"There's somebody here! Who is it? Show yourself!" shouted one of the men. Neither Goon nor Fatty made any movement, and all the wax figures stared stolidly at the group of men.

"It's creepy in here, with all those figures looking at us," said the first man. "But one of them's real! No doubt about that! Come on – we'll soon find out. I've got a torch."

Fatty's heart beat fast. He hoped and hoped that the men would find Goon before they found him. But most unfortunately Fatty was in the front row, and Goon wasn't.

One of the men had a powerful torch. He walked over to Nelson and flashed it in his face. Nelson stared unblinkingly in front of him. "He's wax all right," said the man, and passed to the next figure, a tall soldier. He flashed the torch in his face.

The soldier didn't make a movement at all. It was obvious that he was wax, for there was a little crack down one cheek, where he had once struck his face, when being carried from one place to another.

One after another the wax figures had the torch flashed into their faces, and one after another they stared unblinkingly past the man's head. Fatty began to tremble a little. Would he be able to stare without blinking too? He hoped so.

His turn came. The torch was flashed suddenly in his face, and the boy could not help a sudden blink. His eyes did it automatically, although he did his best not to. He hoped the man hadn't noticed. But there was something about Fatty's bright, shining, living eyes that caught the man's attention at once, as well as the blink. He grabbed at Fatty's arm, and felt it to be warm and soft.

"Here he is!" he said. "Here's the spy. Standing here staring at us, listening to everything!"

Poor Fatty was dragged down off his steps and pulled into the middle of the hall. He was frightened, but he meant to put a bold face on it.

"Who are you?" said the first man, and shone his torch into Fatty's face.

"Napoleon," said Fatty, trying to brave things out. "Just doing it for a joke!"

"He's only a boy," said one of the men, pulling off Napoleon's hat. "How old are you?"

"Fourteen," said Fatty.

The men stared at him. "What are we going to do with him?" said one. "Can't take him off in the car with us – too risky. And we can't waste time dumping him anywhere, because if we're not on time with this job,

116

we'll fail. What he wants is a jolly good questioning and a good thrashing, and he'll get it – but not now. It's time we went."

"We'll be back here again tonight with the stuff," said another man. "We'll tie him up, gag him, put him into the cupboard over there, and lock him in. He can't give the game away then. We'll deal with him when we come back. He can't know anything about the job to-night, except what he's just heard, so he won't have warned any one."

"Right," said the other men, and then began a bad time for poor Fatty. He was rolled up in a curtain, with his hands and feet tied, and a big handkerchief was bound across his mouth. Then he was popped into the cupboard with Napoleon, and the door was shut and locked on him.

His only comfort was that Mr. Goon was still there, posing stolidly, quite unsuspected. As soon as the men had got away, Goon would surely come to his rescue and untie him. Then he, Fatty would be in at the last, after all.

He could hear nothing in the cupboard. He did not hear the men go out of the hall and lock the door. He did not see Goon wait on his step for a few moments and then relax and give a deep sigh. Mr. Goon had had a most surprising and unpleasant time himself from the moment he had sneezed to the moment the men had at last gone.

When he had sneezed, he had felt certain that the men would search the figures and find him. He had no idea at all, of course, that Fatty had been one of the figures too. When the boy had been found and hauled off his stand, Mr. Goon's eyes had almost fallen out of his head.

What – somebody else in the hall – somebody who must have been there when Mr. Goon himself had come in and changed places with the wax policeman? Who was it!

Mr. Goon recognized Fatty's voice as soon as the boy had spoken. He went purple with rage. That interfering boy again! So he, like Goon himself, had read the secret message – and he hadn't told the police. The bad, wicked ... well, words failed Mr. Goon as he stood there thinking about Fatty.

The policeman shook when he thought that the men would probably find him next. When they did not think of looking any further, his heart beat a little less fast. Well, serve that boy right, if he got caught! He deserved to! Keeping information from the police! Mr. Goon's face went red again.

He had been so very pleased with himself at thinking of this idea – posing as the wax policeman, and listening in to the gang and their plans. Well, he knew a lot now, he did – and if only those men would go off to the job and leave him alone, he'd soon do a spot of telephoning, and arrange to catch them all neatly – redhanded, too! Mr. Goon glowed when he thought of it.

But the men hadn't gone yet. They were tying up that fat boy – hadn't even given him a clip over the ear, as Mr. Goon would himself have very much liked to do. The policeman watched with pleased eyes the efficient way in which the men rolled Fatty up in the curtain, his hands and legs well and truly bound, and a handkerchief over his mouth. Ha! That was the way to treat people like Fatty!

Mr. Goon watched the men pop Fatty into the cupboard and turn the key on him. Good! Now that boy was properly out of the way. If only the men would go, Mr. Goon could step down and get busy. He smiled as he thought of how busy he would get. Inspector Jenks would be surprised at his news. Yes, and pleased, too.

The door closed and the men were gone. Mr. Goon heard the sound of a car starting up. He thought it would be safe to step down into the hall, and he stood there, looking round, feeling extremely pleased with himself.

Fatty was struggling hard in the cupboard. He had read books that told him the best way to wriggle free of bonds, but, except that he had managed to get his mouth away from the handkerchief, he wasn't having much luck with his hands and feet! He did all the things the books had advised him to, but it was no good. He couldn't get his hands free.

In his struggles, he fell against Napoleon, and that gentleman over-balanced, and struck his head against the back of the cupboard. He then rolled on to Fatty, who yelled.

Mr. Goon, about to open the door to go out, heard the yell. He paused. He didn't mean to set Fatty free. Not he! That boy had got what he deserved, at last, and he, Mr. Goon, wasn't going to rob him of it. No – let him stay in the cupboard and think about things. Maybe he'd think it was best not to interfere with the Law again.

But when Napoleon fell with such a crash, Mr. Goon felt a stirring of his conscience. Suppose that boy was being suffocated? Suppose that handkerchief stopped his breathing? Suppose he'd wriggled about, and fallen and hurt himself? He was a friend of the Inspector's, wasn't he, though goodness knew why the Inspector should bother himself with a boy like that. Still. ...

Mr. Goon thought he might spare half a minute to investigate. But he wasn't going to unlock that cupboard. No, not he! He wasn't going to have that there boy rushing out on him, all untied, and playing some more of his tricks. No, Fatty was safer locked up in a cupboard.

So Mr. Goon went cautiously to the cupboard and knocked smartly on the door. Fatty's struggles ceased at once.

"Who's that?"

"Mr. Goon," said the policeman.

"Thank goodness!" said Fatty fervently. "Unlock the door and untie me, Mr. Goon. We've work to do! Have those men gone?"

Mr. Goon snorted. Did this fat boy really think he was going to let him help him! After he had deliberately not told him about that secret message, too!

"You're all right in there," said Mr. Goon, "you don't want to come messing about with thieves and robbers, you don't!"

Fatty couldn't believe his ears. Did Mr. Goon really mean he was going to leave him there, in the cupboard, when all the fun was going on? He wriggled about in agony at the thought, and spoke beseechingly.

"Mr. Goon! Be a sport! Unlock the door and let me out!"

"Why should I?" demanded Mr. Goon. "Did you tell me about that secret message? No, you didn't. And I know your parents wouldn't want you mixed up in this business tonight, see? They'll thank me for leaving you here. I'll come and get you later, when we've done all the arresting and everything."

Fatty was desperate. To think of Goon doing it all, whilst he was shut up in this smelly cupboard!

"Mr. Goon! Don't be mean. It was *your* sneeze gave the show away – and instead of catching *you*, they caught *me*. It's not fair."

Mr. Goon laughed. It was rather a nasty laugh. Fatty's heart sank when he heard it. He knew then that the policeman meant to leave him where he was. He could make all kinds of excuses for it – that he hadn't time to free Fatty – that he meant to come back almost at once – anything would do. Blow Mr. Goon!

"Well – see you later," said Mr. Goon, and he walked over to the door. Fatty groaned. Now he would have to stay in the cupboard till the fun was over. It was too bad. After all his fine plans, too! What would Inspector Jenks say? He would be very pleased with Goon, who certainly had used his brains in this Mystery, and worked hard on it.

Poor Fatty! He lay in the cupboard in great discomfort, with rope biting into his wrists and ankles. It was all Goon's fault. What did he want to go and sneeze like that for, and give the game away? He had come out of it very well himself – but he had messed everything up for poor old Fatty.

Suddenly Fatty heard a slight sound and he pricked his ears up. It sounded like the window opening. Was there somebody coming in? Was one of the gang coming back?

Then Fatty heard a low voice – a voice he knew very well indeed.

"Fatty! Are you here anywhere? Fatty!"

It was Larry! Fatty's heart beat for joy and he struggled to a sitting position in the cupboard. "Larry! I'm locked up in the cupboard where we put Napoleon! Let me out! Quick, let me out!"

Mr. Goon Gets a Few Shocks

Larry rushed over to the cupboard. The key was still in the lock. He turned it and the door opened. And there was poor Fatty, still wrapped up in the curtain.

"Fatty! What's happened?" cried Larry. "Are you hurt?"

"Not a bit – except that my wrists and ankles are aching with the rope round them," said Fatty. "Got a knife, Larry? Cut the rope."

Larry cut the ropes, and soon Fatty was unwrapping himself from the curtain. He tossed it into a corner with the cut ropes. He took off Napoleon's uniform, and put on his own clothes. Then he shut and locked the cupboard door.

"Oh Larry!" he said, "wasn't I glad to hear your voice! But don't let's talk here. Let's get back home, quick!"

"My people think I'm in bed," said Larry. "I'll come to your house, if you like. Your people won't be there, will they? Come on."

"Right. We'll tell about everything when we get back," said Fatty.

They made their way back over the fields as fast as they could, though poor Fatty's ankles were painfully swollen now, through being so tightly bound. They soon got to Fatty's house and let themselves in cautiously. They went up to his room and Fatty flung himself on the bed, rubbing his ankles ruefully.

"Larry! How did you manage to come back and rescue me?" he asked. "I'd have been there for hours, if you hadn't. That beast Goon wouldn't let me out. Now – you tell me your story first."

"There isn't really anything to tell," said Larry. "I went back home and told Daisy all we'd done. And then, about half-past nine, when I was in bed, Pip turned up, and threw stones at my window."

"Whatever for?" said Fatty.

"Well, Bets sent him," said Larry. "Pip said she was awfully upset, and wouldn't go to sleep, and kept crying and saying she knew you had got into danger. You know the silly feelings Bets gets sometimes. She's only a baby."

"So Pip, thinking it would be fun to hear how you'd got on, dressing me up as Napoleon, told Bets he'd go round and see you," said Fatty. "It would make Bets feel better, and be a bit of excitement for old Pip. I see that – but what made you come along down to the Waxwork Hall?"

"I don't exactly know," said Larry. "You know, once before Bets got the idea that you were in danger, and it turned out she was right. And I just thought – well, I thought it might be a good idea if I slipped down to the Waxwork Hall and just had a snoop round to see what was happening."

"Golly! I'm glad Bets had one of her feelings," said Fatty thankfully. "And I'm glad you came down, Larry, old boy."

"So am I," said Larry. "When I got there, the Hall was in darkness and there was nobody about at all. So

I opened that window, got in, and called your name. That's all."

There was a silence. Fatty suddenly looked extremely gloomy. "What's up?" said Larry. "You haven't told me what happened yet – or why you got locked up. Were you discovered after all?"

Fatty began his tale. Larry listened in astonishment. So Goon had been there too! When Fatty came to Goon's sneeze, and related how he, Fatty, had been caught because of it, and not Goon, Larry was most sympathetic.

"Poor old Fatty! So Goon got all the information, left you there, the beast, and has gone to do the arresting and reporting. Quite a busy evening for him!"

"He said he'd come back and let me out of that cupboard when the fun was over," said Fatty, beginning to grin. "He'll be surprised to find I'm gone, won't he?"

"He will," said Larry. "He won't know what's happened. Let's pretend to him that we don't know where you are, shall we? We'll go and ask him about you tomorrow – he'll have twenty fits if he thinks you've vanished. He won't know *what* to think!"

"And he'll feel most uncomfortable because he'll know he jolly well ought to have let me out," said Fatty. "Well, I'm going to bed, Larry. You'd better go and get some sleep too. Oh, I do feel so disappointed – after all our work and disguises and plans – for Goon to solve the Mystery and get all the credit!"

The boys parted and Larry ran swiftly home. He wondered what Goon was doing. He thought about the Castleton Mansion and wondered if the thieves were at work – if the house was being quietly surrounded – if Goon was doing some arresting. Well, maybe it would all be in the papers tomorrow.

Goon had certainly done some good work that night. He had surrounded the mansion with men whilst the thieves were actually inside. He had arrested all four of them – although one, alas, had got away in the struggle – and Goon was feeling very pleased with himself indeed. Not a doubt of that.

It wasn't until past midnight that Mr. Goon suddenly remembered that he had left Fatty locked up in the cupboard in the Waxworks Hall.

"Drat that boy!" he thought. "I could go to bed now, and sleep easy, if it wasn't for getting him out of that cupboard. He's had a nice long time there to think over all his misdeeds, he has. Well, I'd better get along and let him out – and give him a few good words of advice too. He's missed all the fun this time – and *I've* solved this Mystery, not him! Ha!"

Mr. Goon cycled down to the Waxworks Hall and, leaving his bicycle outside, went into the Hall. He switched on his torch and walked to the cupboard. He rapped smartly on it.

"Hey, you!" he said. "Ready to be let out yet? We've done everything, and now that the fun's over, you can come along out!"

There was no answer. Mr. Goon rapped loudly again, thinking that Fatty had gone to sleep. But still there was no answer. A little cold feeling crept round Mr. Goon's heart. Surely that boy was all right?

Hurriedly Mr. Goon turned the key in the lock and opened the door. He shone his light into the cupboard. Napoleon looked back at him, standing there in his under-garment – but no Fatty! Mr. Goon's hands began to tremble. Where was that boy? He couldn't get out of a locked cupboard! Or could he? Mr. Goon remembered how Fatty had apparently passed mysteriously through a locked door in the last Mystery.

Mr. Goon poked Napoleon in the ribs to make sure he was wax, and not Fatty. Napoleon did not flinch. He looked straight at Mr. Goon. Yes, he was wax all right.

Mr. Goon shut the door, puzzled and upset. Now where was that boy? Had somebody carried him off? He had seen him bound and gagged, so he couldn't have escaped by himself. Well, then, what had happened?

Mr. Goon went home slowly, pedalling with heavy feet. He ought to have let that boy free before he had gone after the gang. Suppose he didn't turn up in the morning? What explanation could he give to the Inspector? He was seeing him at ten o'clock.

Mr. Goon gave a heavy sigh. He had been looking forward to that interview – now he wasn't so sure. That fat boy was very friendly with the Inspector. If it came out that anything had happened to him, Inspector Jenks might ask some very very awkward questions. Drat the boy!

Fatty slept soundly that night, tired out with his adventures. Mr. Goon slept too, but not so soundly. He dreamt about his great success in arresting the gang – but every time he was about to receive words of praise from the Inspector, Fatty came into the dream, tied up, begging for help. It was most disturbing, because he woke Mr. Goon up each time, and then he found it hard to go to sleep again.

At nine o'clock the Five Find-Outers were all together in Pip's garden, going over and over the happenings of the night before. All of them were most indignant with Goon for leaving Fatty in the cupboard.

"We're going to make him think Fatty's been spirited away," said Larry, with a grin. "We'll wait about the village for him, and each time he passes any of us we'll ask him if he's heard anything of Fatty."

So, at half-past nine the children, with the exception of Fatty, of course, hung about near Goon's house, waiting for him to come out. Larry was at the corner, Pip was near the house, and Daisy and Bets were not far off.

Larry gave a whistle when he saw Goon coming out, wheeling his bicycle, ready to ride over to see the Inspector. He looked very smart indeed, for he had brushed his uniform, cleaned his belt and helmet and shoes, and polished his buttons till they shone. He was the very picture, he hoped, of a Smart Policeman Awaiting Promotion.

"I say, Mr. Goon!" called Pip, as the policeman prepared to mount his bicycle. "Do you know where our friend, Frederick, is?"

"Why should I?" scowled Mr. Goon, but his heart sank. So that boy had vanished!

"Well, we just wondered," said Pip. "I suppose you haven't seen him at all?"

Mr. Goon couldn't say that. He mounted his bicycle and rode off, his face red. He hoped that boy Fatty wasn't going to cause a lot of trouble, just as he, Goon, had got things going so very nicely.

He passed Daisy and Bets. Daisy called out. "Oh, Mr. Goon! Have you seen Fatty? Do tell us if you have!"

"I don't know where he is," said Mr. Goon desperately, and cycled on. But at the corner, there was Larry!

"Mr. Goon! Mr. Goon! Have you seen Fatty? Do you know where he is? Do you think he's disappeared? Mr. Goon, do tell us where he is. Have you locked him up?"

"Course not!" spluttered Mr. Goon. "He'll turn up. He'll turn up like a bad penny, you may be sure!"

He rode on, feeling most uncomfortable. Where *could* the boy be? Had that thief who escaped gone back to the Hall, and taken Fatty? No, that couldn't be, surely. But WHERE WAS that boy?

The Inspector was waiting for Mr. Goon in his office. On his desk were various reports of the happenings of the night before, sent in, not only by Mr. Goon, but by two other policemen who had helped in the arrests, and by plain-clothes detectives who had also been on the case.

He also had reports on what the three prisoners had said when questioned. Some smart work had been done, there was no doubt about that – but something was worrying the Inspector.

Mr. Goon saw it as soon as he got into the office. He had hoped and expected to find his superior officer full of smiles and praise. But no – the Inspector looked rather solemn, and a bit worried. Why?

"Well, Goon," said the Inspector, "some good work appears to have been done on this case. But it's a pity about the pearls, isn't it?"

Mr. Goon gaped. "The pearls, sir? What about them? We've got them, sir – took them off one of the gang."

"Ah, but you see – they are not the stolen pearls," said the Inspector gently. "No, Goon – they are just a cheap necklace the man was going to give his girl! The *real* pearls have vanished!"

The Mystery is not yet Ended

Mr. Goon's mouth opened and shut like a goldfish. He simply couldn't believe his ears.

"But, sir – we got the thieves red-handed. And the one that escaped was only the one on guard in the garden, sir. He hadn't anything to do with the thieving. It was the three upstairs who did that – and we've got them."

"Yes, you've got them, and that was a very good bit of work, as I said," said the Inspector. "But I'm afraid, Goon, that one of the upstairs thieves, when he knew the game was up, simply threw the pearls out of the window to the man below. He must have pocketed them, and then, when he was arrested, struggled so violently that he managed to escape – *with* the pearls. Pity, isn't it?"

Mr. Goon was most dismayed. True, they had got three of the gang – but the pearls were gone. He had waited to catch the men red-handed – and actually let them take the pearls, because he felt so certain he could get them back, when the men were arrested – and now, after all, the robbery had been successful. One of the gang had got them, and would no doubt get rid of them in double quick time.

"It's – it's most unfortunate, sir," said poor Mr. Goon.

"Well – let's hear your tale," said the Inspector. "You only had time to send in a very short report – what's all this about posing as a waxwork?"

Mr. Goon was proud of this bit, and he related it all in

129

full to the interested Inspector. But when he came to the part where he had sneezed, and the men had caught Fatty, instead of himself, Inspector Jenks sat up straight.

"Do you mean to tell me that Frederick Trotteville was there?" he said. "Posing too? What as?"

"Napoleon, sir," said Goon. "Interfering as usual. That boy can't keep his nose out of things, he can't. Well sir, when the men had gone to do the robbery, I crept out after them, and I went to the telephone box and . . ."

"Wait a bit, wait a bit," said the Inspector. "What happened to Frederick?"

"Him? Oh well – nothing much," said Goon, trying to gloss over this bit as quickly as possible. "They just tied him up a bit, sir, and chucked him into a cupboard. They didn't hurt him. Of course, if they'd started any rough stuff with him, I'd have gone for them, sir."

"Of course," said the Inspector gravely. "Well I suppose you went and untied him and let him out of the cupboard before you rushed off to telephone."

Mr. Goon went rather red. "Well, sir – to tell you the truth, sir, I didn't think I had the time – and also, sir, it was a dangerous business last night, and I didn't think that boy ought to be mixed up in it. He's a terror for getting into the middle of things, sir, that boy is, and . . ."

"Goon," said the Inspector, and the policeman stopped abruptly and looked at his superior. He was looking very grave. "Goon. Do you mean to say you left the boy tied up in a locked cupboard? I can hardly believe it of you. What time did you let him out?"

Mr. Goon swallowed nervously. "I went back, sir, about midnight – and I unlocked the cupboard door, sir – and – and the cupboard was empty."

"Good heavens!" said the Inspector, startled. "Do you know what had happened to Frederick?"

"No, sir," said Mr. Goon. The Inspector reached out for one of his five telephones.

"I must ring his home to see if he is all right," he said.

Mr. Goon looked more downcast than ever. "He's – well, he seems to have vanished, sir," he said. The Inspector put down the telephone, and stared at Mr Goon.

"Vanished! What do you mean? This is very serious indeed."

"Well, Sir – all I know is that the other kids – the ones he's always with – they keep on asking me if I know where their friend is," said Mr. Goon desperately. "And if they don't know – well, he might be anywhere!"

"I must look into the matter at once," said the Inspector. "I'll get into touch with his parents. Now finish your story quickly, so that I can get on to this matter of Frederick Trotteville at once."

So poor Mr. Goon had to cut short his wonderful story, and blurt out quickly the rest of the night's happenings. He felt very down in the mouth as he cycled back home. The pearls had gone after all! What a blow! And now this wretched boy had disappeared, and there would be no end of a fuss about him. Privately Mr. Goon thought it would be a very good thing if Fatty disappeared for good. Oh, why hadn't he let him out of that cupboard last night? He had known that he ought to – but it had seemed such a very good way of paying out that interfering boy!

Where could Fatty be? Mr. Goon pondered the matter deeply as he turned into the village street. Had the escaped thief gone back to the Hall, and taken Fatty prisoner, meaning to hold him up for ransom, or something? Mr. Goon went cold at the thought. If such a thing happened, he would be held up to scorn by every one for not having freed Fatty when he could.

He was so deep in thought that he did not see a small dog run at his bicycle. He wobbled, and fell off, landing with a bump on the road. The dog flew round him in delight, barking lustily.

"Clear-orf!" shouted Mr. Goon angrily, and suddenly recognized Buster. "Will you clear-orf!"

He looked round to see who was in charge of Buster – and his mouth fell wide open. He was so astonished that he couldn't get up, but went on sitting down in the road, with Buster making little darts at him.

Fatty was standing there, grinning down at him. *Fatty!* Mr. Goon stared at him. Here he'd been reporting to the Inspector that Fatty had vanished – and the Inspector had gone all hot and bothered about it – and now here was that same boy, grinning down at him, large as life and twice as natural.

"Where've you been?" said Mr. Goon at last, feebly pushing Buster away.

"Home," said Fatty. "Why?"

"*Home?*" said Mr. Goon. "You've been at home? Why, the others kept asking me where you were, see? And I reported your disappearance to the Inspector. He's going to start searching for you."

"But Mr. Goon – why?" asked Fatty innocently. "I'm here. And I got home all right last night, too. All the same, it was jolly mean of you to leave me in that cupboard. I shan't forget that in a hurry."

Mr. Goon got up. "How did you get out of that there cupboard?" he asked. "All tied up you were, too. Do you mean to say you untied yourself, and unlocked

132

Fatty was standing there, grinning down at him

that cupboard and got out all by yourself?"

"You never know, do you?" said Fatty. "Well so long, Mr. Goon – and do telephone the Inspector to tell him not to start searching for me. I'll be at home if he wants me!"

He went off with Buster, and poor Mr. Goon was left to cycle home, his head spinning. "That boy! First he's locked up, then he disappears, then he comes back again – and nobody knows how or when or why." Mr. Goon couldn't make head or tail of it.

He didn't enjoy ringing up the Inspector and reporting that he had just met Fatty.

"But *where* had he been?" said the Inspector, puzzled. "Where was he last night?"

"Er – at home, sir," said poor Mr. Goon. "It was the other children put me off, sir – asking me if I knew where he was, and all that, sir."

The Inspector put down his receiver with an impatient click. Really, Goon was too idiotic at times! The Inspector sat looking at his telephone, thinking deeply. He had had reports from all kinds of people about this Case – but not from one person, who appeared to know quite a lot about it – and that was Master Frederick Trotteville! The Inspector made another telephone call. Fatty answered it.

"I want you to cycle over here this morning and answer a few questions, Frederick," said the Inspector. "Come straight along now."

So, with Buster in his basket, Fatty rode off to the next town, wondering a little fearfully what the inspector wanted to know. Would he think he had been mixing himself up in this Mystery a bit too much? He had warned the Find-Outers not to get mixed up, because it might be dangerous.

The Inspector was friendly, but business-like, and he listened to the whole of Fatty's tale with the greatest interest, especially to the tale of Fatty's various disguises.

"Most interesting," he said. "You've got a gift for that kind of thing, I can see. But don't over-do it. Now – you've heard all about the arrests, I suppose?"

"I only know what's in the paper this morning, sir," said Fatty. "I knew it was no good asking Mr. Goon anything. I'm a bit fed up that he managed the Mystery after all, whilst I was locked up in the cupboard."

"He should have let you out," said the Inspector shortly. "Very remiss of him. Not the kind of thing I expect from a police officer. Well, Frederick, three arrest were made – as you know – but the man on guard in the garden below escaped. And, most unfortunately, he appears to have escaped with the Castleton pearls!"

"But the papers said they were found in one of the arrested men's pockets!" said Fatty.

"We've got later news," said Inspector Jenks. "Those pearls were only cheap ones, bought by one of the men as a gift for his wife – or stolen from somewhere else probably. They're only worth a few pounds. The real pearls have gone."

"I see," said Fatty, and he cheered up considerably. "So – the Mystery isn't quite over, sir. We've got to find out where the pearls are? Can you find the man who escaped, do you think? He might split, and tell where he put the pearls."

"We *have* got him," said the Inspector grimly. "The news came in ten minutes ago. But he hadn't got the pearls, and won't say where he's put them. But we happen to know that Number Three of the gang is usually the one who disposes of the stolen jewels – and its likely that this fellow we've just arrested has put the pearls in some agreed place, for Number Three, whoever he is, to fetch when all the hue and cry dies down."

"You don't know who Number Three is, do you sir?" asked Fatty.

"Haven't any idea," said the Inspector. "We more or less had our suspicions of the other four – but Number Three we've never been able to guess at. Now, Frederick, I'm not altogether pleased at the way you mixed yourself up in this, when I warned you not to, because it was dangerous – now you just see if you can't solve the rest of the Mystery, and find those pearls before Number Three does. There's no danger now – so you Five Find-Outers can go ahead."

"Yes, sir," said Fatty, looking rather subdued. "We'll do our best. We've got just a few things to go on. I'll work them out and see what can be done. Thanks for giving us a chance to solve the Mystery of the Missing Pearls! Good-bye, sir!"

Number Three Again

Fatty went straight to Pip's. He felt sure he would find the rest of the Find-Outers there, waiting for him. They were outside the summer-house, making Larry tell them over and over again all that had happened.

"Here's Fatty!" cried Bets. "What did the Inspector say, Fatty? Wasn't he angry with Goon for leaving you in that cupboard?"

"He wasn't very pleased with him – at least he didn't *sound* very pleased," said Fatty. "He didn't sound very pleased with me either! Seemed to think I oughtn't to have got so mixed up in this Mystery. But how *could* I keep out of it?"

"I expect he thought it was dangerous," said Bets, "and so it was, last night. Oh, Fatty, I knew you were in danger. I really, really did."

"Good old Bets!" said Fatty, giving her a hug. "I'm jolly glad you had one of your funny feelings about me – if you hadn't sent Pip to Larry, and Larry hadn't come along to the Waxworks Hall, goodness knows how long I'd have been shut up in that cupboard. By the way – the Mystery is still not *quite* ended!"

Every one sat up at once. "What do you mean?" said Daisy.

Fatty explained about the missing pearls and Number Three. "The Inspector thinks that Number Five, who escaped with the pearls last night, had time to put them in some safe place, before he was caught this morning. He will probably try and get a message to Number Three – the gang member who wasn't there last night and so is still at large – and till Number Three gets that message about the pearls and finds them, *any* one might find them! And it's up to us to do it!"

"I see," said Larry slowly. "But how in the world can any one find them if they don't even know where to look? It's impossible."

"Nothing's impossible to a really good detective," said Fatty. "I agree that it's a frightfully difficult mystery to solve – but I think if only we can get hold of Number Three somehow, and shadow him, he might lead us to the necklace!"

"What do you mean — shadow him?" asked Bets.

"Follow him, silly — always keep him in sight," said Pip. "Spot where he goes, or where he hangs about. He's sure to hang about the place where the pearls are, waiting for a chance to get them."

"That's right," said Fatty. "The thing is — *who* is Number Three and how can we get hold of him?"

There was a silence. Nobody knew the answer.

"What do we know about Number Three?" said Fatty, considering. "We know he rides a bike that has a hooter on it. We know he has odd eyes, one blue and one brown. And we know he rows a boat. I rather think, as we've seen him in Peterswood twice that he must live here."

There was another silence. None of the things they knew about the odd-eyed man seemed to be of any help in finding him. Then Pip suddenly gave an exclamation.

"I think I know what to do!"

"What?" said every one eagerly.

"Well, we're sure that Number Five hid the pearls somewhere, and we're pretty certain he'll get a message to Number Three, *some*how — has probably sent one already, in case he himself got caught by the police and put into prison. Now who would he send that message to, to deliver to Number Three?"

"The old man, Johnny, of course!" said Fatty. "He's the one they always use, apparently, when they want to send messages to one another. So — if we watch old Johnny again — sooner of later we'll see Number Three go quietly up to him. . . ."

"Sit down beside him — and receive the message!" said Larry. "And if we shadow him, after that, we shall spot where he goes. Maybe he'll lead us straight to the necklace!"

Every one felt much more cheerful and hopeful. "That's a brain-wave of yours, Pip," said Fatty. "I'm surprised I didn't think of it myself. Very good."

All the Find-Outers loved a word of praise from their leader. Pip went quite red with pleasure.

"I suppose that means we must go and sit in that smelly little lemonade shop again," said Daisy. Fatty considered.

"Only one of us had better shadow Number Three closely," he said. "If he sees five of us tailing him he's bound to get a bit suspicious. I'll do the shadowing – if you don't mind, Pip, though it *was* your idea – and you can all follow me at a safe distance."

"I don't mind a bit," said Pip generously. "I'm sure you'll be much better at shadowing than I shall. Where will you wait? And shall we have bikes or not?"

"Better have bikes," said Larry. "He was on a bike last time he went up to the old man. If he's walking we can always leave our bicycles somewhere, and walk after him."

"Yes, that's a sound idea," said Fatty. "What's the time? Almost dinner-time. The old fellow doesn't come out till the afternoon, so we'll meet just before two, at the bottom of my lane, with bikes."

"But, Fatty, do you think the old man will come out and sit on your seat, after your warning, and after what he will have read in the papers today?" asked Larry. "Won't he be afraid?"

"Yes, probably he will," said Fatty. "But if he has a message to deliver, I think he'll risk it. I bet the gang pay him well for this go-between business."

Now that there was something to do again the Find-Outers felt very cheerful. They went to their dinners pleased that there was still a Mystery to solve. If only they could find those pearls before Goon did!

Mr. Goon, of course, was exercising his mind too, about the missing pearls. He too knew that if only he could spot Number Three, he might be led to the pearls. But he had not got as far as reckoning out that it would be a good idea to watch old Johnny again, to see if Number Three came to receive a message!

That afternoon four of the Find-Outers sat in the little sweet-shop, on the opposite side of the road to the bench where the old man so often sat. Fatty was not with them. He was leaning against a tree not far off, apparently deep in a paper, his bicycle beside him. He was watching for the old man to come. How he hoped he would!

The bicycles belonging to the others were piled against the side of the sweet-shop. The four children in the shop were eating ices, and watching the bench opposite as keenly as Fatty was.

Some one came shuffling round the corner. Hurrah! It was the old man, complete with sniffle and pipe and cough. He sat himself down gingerly on the bench with a little groan, just exactly as Fatty used to do.

Then he bent himself over his stick-handle and seemed to go to sleep. The children waited, whilst their ices melted in the saucers. Had Johnny got a message to deliver from Number Five to Number Three?

A noise made them jump violently. It was the sound of a hooter! Fatty jumped too. He lifted his head cautiously from his paper, and saw a man riding down

140

the High Street on a bicycle. It had a hooter instead of a bell.

The man rode to the bench, hooted, and got off his bicycle. He stood his machine against the kerb and went to sit down on the bench close to the old man.

The old fellow did not even look up. How would he know if it was Number Three or not then? He was deaf and would not hear a whisper. Fatty puzzled his brains to think.

"Of course!" he thought suddenly. "That loud hooter always tells the old man when Number Three is coming to sit on the bench beside him. Of course! Gosh, that's clever."

The old man took absolutely no notice of the other man. Fatty watched very carefully, but he could not see any movement of the old man's mouth, nor could he see the giving of any paper-message.

For a few moments the two men sat together, and then old Johnny sat up a little straighter, and began to draw patterns in the dust with the end of his stick. Fatty watched more carefully to see if the old man was talking, under cover of his movements. But he could not make out that he was – unless he could talk without moving his lips, as a ventriloquist can!

After a minute or two the other man got up and went to his bicycle. He got on it, hooted, and rode slowly over to the sweet-shop. The four children in there stiffened with excitement. What was he coming over there for?

Bets gave a gasp as he came in, and Pip kicked her under the table, afraid she might give them away. Bets took one look at the man and then began to finish her ice, making rather a noise with her spoon.

"Box of matches, please," said the man, and put a
141

penny down on the counter. Nobody liked to look at him in case he became suspicious of them.

He went out, lighting a cigarette. "He's got odd *eyes!*" said Bets. "He's the one! Hooter on his bike – and odd eyes! Oooh – it's getting exciting."

Fatty, waiting by the tree outside, saw the man go in and out of the shop. The boy folded up his paper quickly, and mounted his bike as the man went swiftly by him. He followed him at a discreet distance, wondering if he had had any message, and if he was going to lead him to the pearls!

"Come on," said Larry, going out of the shop quickly. "We've got to follow too."

The man rode down to the Fair. He wandered round a bit and then went to the Hall of Waxworks. But he only just put his head inside, and came out.

Fatty popped his head inside too, but except that it was full of people looking at the waxworks, there was nothing different to see. Napoleon was dressed and back in his place, and the red-haired boy was relating an extraordinary tale of how, in the night, Napoleon had apparently got out of his place, undressed and put himself to bed in a cupboard.

"Story-teller!" said some listening children. "What a fib!"

"And what's more," said the red-headed boy, thoroughly enjoying himself, "that wax policeman over there – do you see him? Well, *he* got up in the night and went and stood himself behind that curtain. Such goings-on!"

Fatty longed to hear more of this, but the man he was following had gone, and Fatty had to go too, or lose him.

142

The man had put his bicycle beside the hedge and padlocked the back wheel, so Fatty knew he meant to stay around for a while.

The other Find-Outers came up, and Fatty winked at them. "Looks as if we're going to spend an hour or two in the Fair!" he said.

The man wandered about most aimlessly. He didn't even have a ride on the roundabout, or try for a Hoopla gift, or go in a Bumping Car – he just trailed about. Every now and then he passed the Waxworks Hall, and looked inside. But he didn't go in at all. Fatty wondered if he was waiting for somebody to meet him there.

"I don't believe he knows where the pearls are!" thought Fatty. "Or surely he'd go straight to them! My word what a crowd there is at the Fair today!"

The man evidently thought the same. He asked a question about it of the man at the Hoopla stall. "Quite a crowd today! What's up?"

"Oh, it's a trip from Sheepsale, a kind of outing," said the man. "They're going at four o'clock, then the place will empty a bit. Good trade for us, though!"

The man nodded. Then he made his way through the crowd to his bicycle, and unpadlocked it. Fatty followed him. It was clear that the man couldn't do whatever he wanted to do, because the place was too crowded. Probably he would be coming back. It was up to Fatty to follow him. He would leave the others down in the Fair, because he was sure that he and the man would be back there sooner or later, when the trippers had gone.

He had time to give a quick message to Larry. Then off he went over the level-crossing on his bicycle, following the man as closely as he dared. Round the corner they went, the man hooting with his little hooter – parp-parp.

And round the corner on *his* bicycle came Goon! The two almost collided. Goon, who had heard the hooter, glued his eyes on the man at once. Was he Number Three? He must be! He seemed to be the only man within miles who had a hooter on his bicycle, instead of a bell, for some peculiar reason that Goon couldn't guess.

Goon made up his mind to follow Number Three at once, and keep him in sight. Visions of pearl necklaces floated in front of his eyes. Number Three knew where those pearls were, Goon was sure of it. Off he went after Number Three.

And behind him went Fatty, annoyed and angry. Was Goon going to get in first *again*! Goon heard some one behind him and turned. He scowled.

That fat boy again! Was he after Number Three too. "Gah!" said Goon to himself. "The interfering Toad!"

A Nice Long Ride

And now, of course, Mr. Goon spoilt simply everything! Number Three couldn't possibly help guessing that he was being shadowed by the fat, panting policeman! For one thing, Goon didn't keep a fair distance away, but pedalled closely to Number Three's bicycle – so close to it that if Number Three had to brake suddenly, his "shadow" would almost certainly bump into him!

Fatty cycled on, some way behind the other two,

thinking hard. It was too bad of Old Clear-Orf to butt in like this, just as the Find-Outers had really got going again. For one moment Fatty knew what Mr. Goon felt like, when others interfered! He, Fatty, had often interfered with the policeman's working out of a mystery – and now here was Goon doing the same thing. And he'd done it the evening before, too, in the Waxworks Hall. It was most exasperating.

Number Three, giving occasional scowling glances behind him, saw that Goon was hot on his trail. He didn't really need to look round him to see the policeman, because he could hear him well enough too – Goon's puffs and pants were terrific.

A little grin curled the corners of Number Three's lips. Goon wanted a bicycle ride, did he? All right then, he could have it, with pleasure. Number Three would take him for a long, long ride through the countryside, on this hot, sultry afternoon!

Fatty soon began to have an inkling of the way in which Number Three's mind was working, for the man suddenly seemed to have a tremendous desire to cycle up all the steep hills it was possible to find.

He was a strong, muscular fellow, and he sailed up the hills easily enough – but poor Goon found it terribly hard work, and Fatty wasn't very happy either. He began to puff too, and to wish that he had given Larry or Pip the job of shadowing this extremely active fellow.

"The wretched man knows that Goon is following him because he suspects him of knowing where the pearls are, and he going to lead him a fine old dance, up hill and down dale!" thought Fatty, his legs going round and round furiously, and the perspiration dripping into his eyes. "He's either going to tire old Goon out, and make him give up – or else he's going to give him the slip somehow."

Still the three went on and on, and Fatty's clothes stuck to him horribly, he was so hot. Number Three didn't seem to tire in the least, and had a most uncanny knowledge of all the nasty little hills in the district. Poor Mr. Goon went from red to scarlet, and from scarlet to purple. He was in his hot uniform, and even Fatty felt a bit sorry for him.

"He'll have a fit if he goes up any more hills at top speed," thought Fatty, wiping his forehead. "So shall I! Golly, I'm absolutely melting. I shall have lost pounds and pounds in weight soon. Phew!"

Mr. Goon was absolutely determined that he wasn't going to be shaken off by Number Three. He knew that Fatty was behind him, and that if he, Mr. Goon, failed in the chase, Fatty would go triumphantly on. So Mr. Goon gritted his big teeth and kept on and on and on.

A big hill loomed up in front. Mr. Goon groaned from the bottom of his heart. Number Three sailed up as usual. Mr. Goon followed valiantly. Fatty, feeling that this was absolutely the last straw, went up it too.

And then he felt a peculiar bumping from his back tyre. He looked down in alarm. Blow, blow, blow! He'd got a puncture!

Poor Fatty. He got off and looked at his tyre. It was absolutely flat. No good pumping it up, because it would be flat again almost at once – and, in any case, if he stopped to pump it up he would lose Number Three and Mr. Goon.

If he had been Bets he would have burst into howls. If he had been Daisy he would have sat on the bank and shed a few quiet tears. If he had been Larry he would have shaken his fist at the tyre and kicked it. If he had been Pip he would probably have yelled at it and then jumped on it in fury. But being Fatty, he did none of these things at all.

He took a quick look up the hill and caught sight of a triumphant Mr. Goon looking back at him with a grin on his face. Then he and Number Three disappeared over the top of the hill. Fatty waved to Goon.

"I wish you a nice long ride!" he said pleasantly, and mopped his forehead. Then he waited for a car to come along over the top of the hill.

It wasn't long before he heard one. It was a lorry, driven by a young man with a cigarette hanging out of the corner of his mouth. Fatty hailed him.

"Hie! Stop a minute, there's a good-chap."

The lorry stopped. Fatty took a half-crown out of his pocket. "Would you mind stopping at the next garage and asking them to send out a taxi for me?" he said. "I've got a puncture, and I'm miles from anywhere, and don't want to have to walk home."

"Bad luck, mate," said the driver. "Where do you live?"

"Peterswood," said Fatty. "I don't know how far I've ridden this afternoon, but I imagine it must be about twenty miles away!"

"Oh, not so far as that, mate!" said the driver. "I'm going near Peterswood. Chuck your bike in the back of the lorry, climb up here beside me – and put your money away! I can give a chap a lift without being paid for it!"

"Oh, thanks awfully," said Fatty, and put away his half-crown. He lifted his bicycle into the lorry, and then climbed up beside the driver. He was very hot and tired, and terribly thirsty, but he chatted away in a friendly manner, glad to have this unexpected lift back.

"Here you are," said the driver, when they had rattled through the countryside for about twenty minutes. "Peterswood is not above a mile from here. You can walk that."

"Very many thanks," said Fatty, and jumped down. He took his bicycle and waved to the departing lorry. Then he walked smartly off in the direction of Peterswood. He went home and put away his punctured bike. His father's bike was in the shed, so Fatty borrowed that, and off he went, quite cheerful, on his way to the Fair to see what the others were doing.

They were wondering what had happened to Fatty. They hadn't liked to leave the Fair, so they had had tea there, and were now conversing with the red-headed boy at the Waxworks, hearing for the twentieth time, the extraordinary tale of Napoleon's escapade in the night.

"Oh, *Fatty*!" cried Bets, when she saw him. "You've come back at last! Whatever happened? And how frightfully hot you look!"

Buster welcomed Fatty uproariously. He had been left behind with Larry, in case Fatty had to do some quick shadowing. Fatty looked at him.

"I feel as if *my* tongue's hanging out like Buster's, I'm so hot and thirsty," he said. "I must have an iced gingerbeer. Come and sit with me whilst I have it, and I'll tell you what's happened!"

"Did Number Three lead you to the missing pearls?" asked Bets excitedly, as Fatty went to the gingerbeer stall. He shook his head.

"Come on over to the grass here," he said, and led the way. He flung himself down and drank his gingerbeer in long, thirsty gulps. "Golly! This is the very best drink I've ever had in my life!"

Soon he was telling the others about the wild-goose chase that Number Three had led both him and Mr. Goon. They listened eagerly. How annoying of Goon to butt in like that! They laughed when they thought of the poor, hot, fat policeman pedalling valiantly up hill and down after Number Three.

"What a shame you had a puncture," said Bets. "Still, Fatty, I'm sure Number Three would never lead you or Goon to where the pearls were, once he knew he was being followed! He might not have known that *you* were shadowing him – but he simply couldn't *help* knowing that Goon was!"

Fatty finished his iced gingerbeer and ordered another. He said he had never been so thirsty in his life. "When I think of poor, hot Goon, pedalling away still for dear life, and feeling as thirsty as I am – well, all I can say is that I'm jolly glad I got a puncture!" said Fatty, drinking again. "I should think Goon will end up somewhere in Scotland, by the time he's finished this bike-ride!"

"All the same," said Larry, "it's a bit sickening that we aren't any nearer solving the mystery of where those pearls are hidden. Instead of the man leading us *to* them – he seems bent on going as far from them as he can!"

"I wonder if that old fellow *did* give him a message," said Pip, frowning. "You're sure you didn't see any sign of a message at all? Let's think now. All that old Johnny did was to mess about in the dust, drawing patterns with his stick. Nothing else."

Fatty was drinking his gingerbeer as Pip said this. He

suddenly choked and spluttered, and Bets banged him on the back. "Whatever's the matter?" she said.

Fatty coughed, and then turned a pair of bright eyes on the Find-Outers. "Pip's hit it!" he said. "What a lot of blind donkeys we are! Of course – *we saw that old chap giving the message to Number Three under our very noses* – and we weren't smart enough to spot it!"

"What do you mean?" said every one, in surprise.

"Well – he must have been writing some kind of message with his stick, in the dust, of course, for Number Three to read!" said Fatty. "And to think it was there for us to read, too, if only we'd gone over and used our eyes. We're bad Find-Outers. Very bad indeed."

The others looked excited. Pip slapped Fatty on the shoulder. "Well, come on, let's go and see if the message is still there, idiot! It might be!"

"It might. But it's not very likely now," said Fatty, getting up. "Still, we'll certainly go and see. Oh – to think we never thought of this before. Where are my brains? They must have melted in this heat!"

The Find-Outers, with Buster in Fatty's basket, set off back to the village street. They came to the bench. It was empty – but obviously people had been sitting there, for there were paper bags strewn about. The children looked eagerly at the dust in front of the seat. Would there still be a message they could read?

Hunt-The-Necklace

There were certainly some marks in the dust, but not many, for somebody's feet had evidently scuffled about just there. Fatty sat himself down in exactly the same place in which the old man had been. He stared hard at the dust.

So did the others. "That looks like a letter W," said Fatty, at last, pointing. "Then there's a letter half rubbed out. And then that looks like an X. Then all the rest of the letters have been brushed out where people have walked on them. Blow!"

"W – something – X," said Larry, who was good at crosswords, with their missing letters. "W – A – X it might be that."

And then exactly the same thought struck all the Find-Outers at the same moment.

"WAXworks! That's what the word was!"

They stared at one another in the greatest excitement. Waxworks! Were the pearls hidden somewhere in the Waxworks Hall? It was a very likely place, a place that all the gang knew well. And Number Three had kept looking in at the door that afternoon.

"He kept peeping in – but he couldn't go and get the pearls, because there were too many people there!" said Fatty. "Golly, we've got the idea now! Now we've only got to go there and hunt, and we'll find the pearls somewhere – in the cupboard, perhaps, or under a floorboard."

"Let's go and look for them straightaway," said Larry, getting up. "Come on."

"We can't very well, under the nose of that redhaired boy," said Fatty. "Still, we'll go down to the Hall anyway." They set off and soon came to the Fair again.

"There's the red-headed boy over there – he's gone to his tea or something," said Bets, pointing. "Has he left the Hall empty for once?"

They hurried to see. There was a badly written notice

stuck on the locked door. "Gone for tea. Back soon."

"Aha!" said Fatty, his eyes gleaming. "This couldn't be better for us. We'll get in at that window, Larry. It's sure to be open still."

It was still unfastened, and the children climbed in excitedly, almost tumbling on to the floor in their eagerness to go hunting for the pearls.

"Behind the curtains, in the cupboards, up the chimney, every place you can think of!" said Fatty, in a thrilled voice. "Go to it, Find-Outers. Solve the mystery if you can!"

Then such a hunt began. Every cupboard, every shelf, every nook and cranny in that Hall were searched by the bright-eyed Find-Outers. Buster, eager to help, though without the faintest idea of what they were looking for, scrabbled about too, having a vague hope that it might be rabbits.

Fatty even examined the floor-boards, but none of them was loose. At last, when it seemed as if every single place had been searched, the five children sat down to rest and discuss the matter.

"I suppose it *is* here, that necklace!" said Daisy. "I'm beginning to think it isn't."

"*I* feel as if I'm playing Hunt-the-Thimble," said Bets. "Where *is* the thimble? It must be in some jolly good place, that necklace!"

Fatty stared at Bets. "Bets," he said, "supposing we went out of the room, and you had to hide a pearl necklace somewhere here, what difficult place would you think of?"

Bets looked round the Hall and considered. "Well, Fatty," she said, "I've always noticed that when people play Hunt-the-Thimble, the most difficult hiding-places to find are the easiest ones really."

"What do you mean?" demanded Pip.

"Well," said Bets, "I remember looking *every*where for the thimble once – and nobody found it – and yet where do you think it was? On Mother's finger!"

Fatty was listening hard to Bets. "Go on, Bets," he said. "Suppose you had to hide that pearl necklace here, in this Hall – where would *you* hide it? It would have to be a good place, easy to get at – and yet one where ordinary people would never dream of looking for a valuable necklace."

Bets considered again. Then she gave a little smile. "Well, *I* know where I'd put it!" she said. "Of course I'd know! And it would be under the noses of every one, and yet nobody would notice it!"

"Where?" cried every one.

"I'll tell you," said Bets. "See Queen Elizabeth over there, in her grand clothes and jewels, standing looking so proud and haughty? Well, I'd put the pearl necklace round her neck with all the other necklaces, of course – and nobody would ever guess that among the false Woolworth ones there was a REAL one!"

Fatty leapt to his feet. "Bets, you're right. I'd got that idea half in my own mind, and now you've said all that, I'm sure you're right! I bet the necklace is there! Clever old Bets!"

They all ran to the stately wax figure of Queen Elizabeth whose neck was hung with brilliant necklaces of all kinds. Among them was a double necklace of beautifully graded pearls, with a diamond clasp – at least, the children felt sure it was a diamond one. Fatty lifted the necklace carefully off the figure's neck, undoing the clasp first.

The pearls shone softly. It was clear even to the children's eyes that they were not cheap ones, bought at a store. They were lovely, really lovely.

"These must be the missing pearls!" said Fatty, exultantly. "They really must! Golly, we've found them. *We've* solved that mystery! What will the Inspector say? Let's go and ring him up."

They climbed out of the window and hurried to their bicycles. Fatty had the wonderful necklace safely in his pocket. He couldn't believe that they really had found it – and in such an easy place too!

"But a jolly clever one," said Fatty. "To think it was under the eyes of scores of people today – and nobody guessed! It was safer on Queen Elizabeth's neck than anywhere else!"

"Look out – there's Goon!" said Larry.

"And Inspector Jenks with him!" cried Bets in delight. "Shall we tell him?"

"Leave it to me," ordered Fatty. "Good evening, Inspector. Come to hunt for the necklace too?"

"Frederick," said the Inspector. "I believe you were bicycling after the member of the gang called Number Three this afternoon, weren't you?"

"Yes, sir," said Fatty. "With Mr. Goon, as well, sir."

"Well, unfortunately he gave Mr. Goon the slip," said the Inspector. "Mr. Goon rang me up, and I came over because it is imperative that we keep an eye on Number Three, if we can, owing to his knowledge of where the pearls are hidden. Did you by any chance see the man, after you had got your puncture?"

"No, sir," said Fatty. "Haven't set eyes on him."

The Inspector gave an annoyed exclamation. "We

must get Number Three. We've found out that he is the ring-leader, and the man we want most of all! And now if he get those pearls, wherever they are, and clears off, sooner or later these burglaries will start all over again. He will find it quite easy to start a new gang."

Mr. Goon looked very down in the mouth. He also looked hot and tired.

"He's a clever fellow, sir," he said to the Inspector. "Very clever. I don't know how he managed to give me the slip, sir."

"Never mind, Mr. Goon," said Fatty comfortingly. "*I* can tell the Inspector where the pearls are, and how you can catch Number Three if you want to."

Mr. Goon stared disbelievingly at Fatty. "Gah!" he said. "You make me tired. Talking a lot of tommy-rot! I don't believe a word of it!"

"What do you mean, Frederick?" said the Inspector, startled.

Fatty drew the pearl necklace out of his pocket. Mr. Goon gasped and his eyes bulged more than ever. The Inspector stared in amazement too. He took the pearls from Fatty. All the children crowded round in excitement.

"Frederick! These *are* the missing pearls! A double row of the very finest graded pearls there are," said the Inspector. "My dear boy – where *did* you get them!"

"Oh – we played a little game of Hunt-the-Thimble with Bets – and she told us where they were," said Fatty, and Mr. Goon gave a disbelieving snort. "They were round Queen Elizabeth's neck, in the Waxworks Hall, Inspector – a very clever place – and Bets thought of it!"

"Certainly a very clever place," said the Inspector, "and a very clever thought of yours, little Bets, if I may say so!" he said, turning to the delighted little girl. "They must have been shining there under the noses of hundreds of people today – and nobody so much as guessed! But now, Frederick – how do you propose that we lay hands on Number Three?"

"Well, sir – he knows that the pearls were hidden in the Waxworks Hall," said Fatty, "and maybe knows too that they were on Queen Elizabeth's neck – so he's bound to go back for them, sir, when every one has gone, and the Hall is dark and empty. Oh, sir – could I come and hide in the Hall tonight when you do your spot of arresting!"

"No," said the Inspector. "I'm afraid not. I'll have three men posted there. See to that straight-away, please, Goon. Er – I'm sure we can congratulate the Find-Outers on solving our problems for us in such a praiseworthy way – don't you think so, Goon?"

Goon murmured something that sounded suspiciously like "Gah!"

"What did you say, Goon?" said the Inspector. "You were agreeing with me, I imagine?"

"Er – yessir, yessir," said Goon hurriedly, and turned a familiar purple. "I'll get the men now, sir."

He hurried off, and the children saw that even the back of poor Goon's neck was bright purple too. The Inspector slipped the pearls into his pocket and beamed all round.

"Well, once more, you've done remarkably well," he said, "though I must confess I was a little annoyed with you, Frederick, for running heedlessly into danger. Still, as usual, you've used your brains, and have helped a great deal. Especially little Bets, if she really did think where the necklace might be."

"Oh, she *did*," said every one, even Pip, and Bets went as red as a tomato with pride. She might be the youngest of the Find-Outers – but she was just as good as any of them!

"Now – I can take it that you will respect my wishes and not go near the Waxworks Hall tonight?" said the Inspector, raising his eyebrows at them all. They nodded vigorously.

"You can trust us, Inspector. But tell us in the morning if you've got Number Three, won't you?" said Fatty.

And in the morning the Find-Outers heard what had happened. Number Three had let himself into the Hall at midnight. He had walked to Queen Elizabeth, and had fumbled at the jewellery round her neck – and just as he was fumbling, out stepped three burly men and caught him!

"Now he's in a cell thinking sadly over his sins," said the Inspector, over the telephone. "We've got the whole gang – and the necklace too. Good work! We certainly couldn't have done without you Find-Outers. What about you all joining my police-force? We could do with you!"

"Oh, how I wish we could!" said Bets, afterwards. "I suppose he didn't really mean it, did he?"

"And now to think we've got to help with our packing and go back to school!" said Pip, in disgust. "After all our fine detective work, we've got to go and learn the chief rivers of the world, and the date when Queen Elizabeth came to the throne, and how much wheat Canada grows, and . . ."

"Never mind — we'll have another Mystery to solve next hols," said Bets happily. "Won't we, Fatty?"

Fatty grinned at her. "I hope so, little Bets," he said. "I really do hope so!"

I hope so too. It would be *most* disappointing if they didn't!

DRAGON BOOKS

The Dragon series is one of the finest Children's Libraries in print today. Enid Blyton, Lewis Carroll, Lady Antonia Fraser, Noel Streatfeild, Christine Pullein-Thompson, Mary O'Hara, show-jumper Pat Smythe and many others are all here to delight every child, whatever the mood or time of day. The Dragon authors represent a charming array of the most creative and time-honoured talents ever at work in the children's field – a pasture of absorbing and intimate pleasure through which wind our chequered Pied Pipers with their ageless tunes and tales, to the joy of millions of Dragon readers. As for Kid's Power – Dragon Books are just the thing to occupy young people finding out perhaps for the first time that peace and quiet can be lovely with a book, and who are beginning to discover for themselves the surprising fun in store for them in the world beyond the family.

If you or your parents have trouble in obtaining titles, please remember that they are available from Cash Sales Dept., P.O. Box 11, Falmouth, Cornwall, at the price shown plus 5p postage.

ENID BLYTON (cont.)

Fifteen-Minute Tales 20p
Twenty-Minute Tales 20p
More Twenty-Minute Tales 20p
Eight O'Clock Tales 20p
The Children's Life of Christ 17p
The Red Storybook 20p
The Yellow Storybook 20p
The Blue Storybook 20p
The Green Storybook 20p
Tales from the Bible 17p

MARY O'HARA

My Friend Flicka – Part 1 20p
My Friend Flicka – Part 2 20p
Thunderhead – Part 2 12p
Thunderhead – Part 3 12p
Green Grass of Wyoming – Part 1 12p
Green Grass of Wyoming – Part 2 12p
Green Grass of Wyoming – Part 3 12p

CHRISTINE PULLEIN-THOMPSON

The Open Gate 17p
The Empty Field 17p
The First Rosette 17p
The Second Mount 17p
The Pony Dopers 12p
For Want of a Saddle 20p
The Impossible Horse 20p

MOLLIE CLARKE
(In Colour)

Rabbit and Fox *and* Skillywidden 25p
Mink and the Fire
and Aldar the Trickster 25p

PAT SMYTHE

A Swiss Adventure 20p
A Spanish Adventure 20p

ANTONIA FRASER

King Arthur and the Knights of the
    Round Table (Illus. by Rebecca
    Fraser) 40p

LEWIS CARROLL

Alice's Adventures in Wonderland
    (Original illus.) 25p
Alice's Adventures Through the
    Looking-Glass (Original illus.) 25p

ARTHUR C. CLARKE

Dolphin Island 12p

NOEL STREATFEILD

The House in Cornwall 17p

. . . and many, many more. Enquire at your local bookshop.